She would [...] **week—superficially a convenient arrangement to suppress scandal, but still his wife.**

They would see this out in *every* way. What had happened in the last two years wasn't Ares's business, but these next few days, she would be his. Only his.

"You will do it, Bethan." He leaned forward, reckless determination pouring through him. "Because if you don't pose as my happily reconciled wife for the next week and come to the gala, then I'll argue that we've been together this whole time. That will reset the clock for our divorce. Two more years tied to me, you ready for that?"

"You're dreaming," Bethan said scathingly, unable to believe her ears. "No one will ever believe we've *not* been separated. I've been living in London."

"And I've made frequent trips to London over the last two years." He smiled at her evilly. "Who's to say you weren't in my bed each and every one of the nights I was there?"

A brand-new and exciting trilogy from USA TODAY bestselling author Natalie Anderson.

Convenient Wives Club

Once bitten... Twice a bride!

Disastrous first marriages taught friends Elodie, Phoebe and Bethan one important lesson. From now on, the only commitment they'll be making is to each other and their friendship. And the only vow they'll be making is *never* to say "I do" again—
for as long as they shall live.

But all three women will be made to
break their promise...

Realizing her parents are forcing her little sister into a convenient marriage, Elodie is determined not to let her sibling suffer the same fate she once had. Her solution? Offering herself to the groom as the bride. The problem? She's got the wrong man!

Their Altar Arrangement

Discovering that the alluring stranger she spent one intoxicating night with is her new boss is only the first of Phoebe's problems. The second? Two pink lines that alter and bind their lives together...permanently!

Boss's Baby Acquisition

Bethan once took a holiday fling too far by marrying her handsome lover. Now it's time to rectify her reckless mistake by returning to Greece to end their farcical marriage. But one slip forces her to remain the billionaire's wife for another week... Allowing their passionate chemistry to reignite!

Greek Vows Revisited

All available now!

GREEK VOWS REVISITED

NATALIE ANDERSON

Harlequin

PRESENTS

If you purchased this book without a cover you should be aware that this book is stolen property. It was reported as "unsold and destroyed" to the publisher, and neither the author nor the publisher has received any payment for this "stripped book."

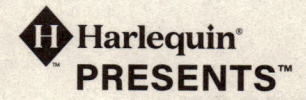

Harlequin® PRESENTS™

ISBN-13: 978-1-335-21329-7

Greek Vows Revisited

Copyright © 2025 by Natalie Anderson

All rights reserved. No part of this book may be used or reproduced in any manner whatsoever without written permission.

Without limiting the author's and publisher's exclusive rights, any unauthorized use of this publication to train generative artificial intelligence (AI) technologies is expressly prohibited.

This is a work of fiction. Names, characters, places and incidents are either the product of the author's imagination or are used fictitiously. Any resemblance to actual persons, living or dead, businesses, companies, events or locales is entirely coincidental.

For questions and comments about the quality of this book, please contact us at CustomerService@Harlequin.com.

TM and ® are trademarks of Harlequin Enterprises ULC.

Harlequin Enterprises ULC
22 Adelaide St. West, 41st Floor
Toronto, Ontario M5H 4E3, Canada
www.Harlequin.com

Printed in Lithuania

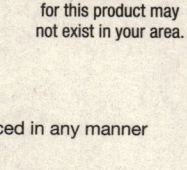

USA TODAY bestselling author **Natalie Anderson** writes emotional contemporary romance full of sparkling banter, sizzling heat and uplifting endings—perfect for readers who love to escape with empowered heroines and arrogant alphas who are too sexy for their own good. When she's not writing, you'll find Natalie wrangling her four children, three cats, two goldfish and one dog...and snuggled in a heap on the sofa with her husband at the end of the day. Follow her at natalie-anderson.com.

Books by Natalie Anderson

Harlequin Presents

The Night the King Claimed Her
The Boss's Stolen Bride
My One-Night Heir

Billion-Dollar Christmas Confessions

Carrying Her Boss's Christmas Baby

Innocent Royal Runaways

Impossible Heir for the King
Back to Claim His Crown

Billion-Dollar Bet

Billion-Dollar Dating Game

Convenient Wives Club

Their Altar Arrangement
Boss's Baby Acquisition

Visit the Author Profile page
at Harlequin.com for more titles.

For Binti, thank you so much for stepping in
and saving me from serious manuscript stress.
I will be forever grateful!

CHAPTER ONE

BETHAN EAGLE PITCHED her smile in that perilously precise point between friendly and firm, inwardly berating herself for the four hundredth time. She *never* should have said yes. She'd regretted it the moment she had and ever since, most especially all through dinner. She'd hoped to extricate herself quickly, but the guy beside her was old-fashioned enough to insist he accompany her home safely—albeit in a fully courteous, not creepy, way. Honestly that made it worse—it wasn't his fault she was an awkward failure. He deserved far better.

Her smile wavered as the car pulled to the kerb. 'You don't need to walk me to the door—'

But he was already out and stepping around to open her door.

'Thanks for seeing me home, you really didn't need to.' Bethan held her bag in front of her and shifted her weight from one foot to the other, battling the urge to flee. 'My flatmate's inside, waiting up. She's been working late with her new job and keeping tabs on me at the same time because I...'

Never date.

Duh, Captain Obvious calling—she'd been beyond

tense the whole time even though it was short—she'd declined dessert and after-dinner drinks and had been a definite 'no' to dancing.

'I've been busy,' she added needlessly. 'Lots of work on as well and...'

And she couldn't stop her mouth from moving—anxiously over-sharing and prolonging this interaction when all she really wanted was to be alone again. She was an idiot. And not ready. *So not ready.* Tonight's test cemented that fact. Her friends Elodie and Phoebe might be ready to date again, but Bethan was officially going to be the life-long loner in their trio.

'Never mind.' She smiled weakly as she finally got a grip on her motor-mouth. 'But I'd better get inside.'

Her patient gentleman of a date shot her an easy smile. 'I enjoyed meeting you tonight, Bethan, I hope we can do this again sometime.'

Really? *Why?* She'd hardly been great company. She'd skittishly jumped from one topic to the next and barely touched her food—literally unable to settle. She swallowed, suddenly realising the man was probably just being polite. 'Um...'

His smile deepened and he stepped back towards the car. 'Call me when you're ready.'

She breathed out, thankful he'd made no attempt to touch her. Yeah, it wasn't a 'kiss goodnight' kind of date, definitely not a 'come in for coffee' one. But she appreciated that he understood that without her having to spell it out.

Of course he did. He was just being polite, remember?

He got back in the car and the ride-share driver restarted the engine and Bethan turned to walk up the short path to the door. Yeah, now she knew. That guy had been nice—exactly the sort of man she *should* date. Perfectly charming. Extremely polite. *Not* some force of nature entirely used to getting his own way. Not a human-form tornado who would sweep her up in his path and spin her around until she dizzily said yes to anything and everything he asked only to then spit her out the second he was done with her. Tonight's date hadn't been *that* kind of man at all. He'd been sweet and attentive and safe. The trouble was she'd had *zero* reaction to him. The only thing she'd felt all night was this relief now he'd left. Beyond that she was dead inside—destroyed by the singular force of nature she'd had the misfortune to meet almost two and a half years ago. Not just meet. *Marry.* Yeah, fool that she was she'd let him ruin her entire romantic future. *No*, she mentally corrected. She wasn't ruined. Just not recovered. *Yet.* Tonight had been too soon. That was all.

She reached the door of the ground-floor flat her friend Phoebe owned. Bethan would be eternally grateful that Phoebe had invited her to share and charged her very little rent for the privilege. She'd met her through her boss, Elodie, and the three had quickly grown close, in part because they had a strong common bond—heartbreak—each having disastrous marriages behind them. While Elodie and Phoebe were both further along their recoveries, they respected Bethan's need not to discuss her past yet. They were supportive and smart and had made her life so different from her lonely, mean-girl-filled school years. They'd become family—not the idealistic perfect family of her foolish, youthful dreams, but actually *real*.

Now she heard the car depart but despite the resulting quiet her tension didn't ease. All night she'd had the oddest feeling someone was watching her and been unable to shake the certainty off. It was probably hyped-up self-consciousness—thinking everyone was watching because this was the first date she'd been on in years. Truthfully it was her first date *ever*, given that with her ex there'd never actually been a date, only intensity. She'd been all in from the moment they'd met. But that prickle sharpened and she glanced back, expecting the street to be empty.

A large black SUV was parked diagonally across from her flat. She'd not noticed it before but as she frowned at it, the rear passenger door opened. Long legs emerged and a tall male frame unfolded with predatory grace.

Bethan's heart contracted. Her lungs crumpled. But it was the complete collapse of her overthinking brain that was the clincher. Words vanished. Her wits paralysed for all eternity. She could barely stand and only stare as Ares Vasiliadis stalked out of the shadows towards her. The downward glow of the streetlight confirmed his identity but she'd known the instant she'd glimpsed his silhouette. Still a force of nature. Still as spellbinding—correction, *stupefying*—as ever. Still lean and lithe and she knew that black suit and brilliant white shirt had been hand-tailored to fit his height and breadth with immaculate perfection.

Despite the faint screams from her neutralised brain, she kept staring. Light stubble emphasised the bold slashes of his chiselled cheekbones. Grey-blue eyes glittered beneath stark brows. Long nose. Wide mouth. His bone structure couldn't be more on point than if he'd been sculpted by Michelangelo himself. It would be a cliché to say he was the walking embodiment of a Greek god, but the reality was the man was the next best thing to an *actual* Greek god. Ares was a billionaire shipping magnate—controller of a massive company that covered all aspects of the seas with a huge merchant fleet as well as ferries for public transport and mega-yachts for the playboys like him. Strong jawed. Strong armed. Strong everything. Her muscles quivered as a very *particular* memory involving his strength shook her. He was powerful. Revered by all. Wanted by all. *Especially* her.

The day they'd met he'd been in a faded grey tee and ripped shorts and she'd been too gauche to know that his watch was one of only ten hand-crafted in the entire world and literally priceless. But tonight, from his gleaming shoes to that perfect suit to that very watch, his attire epitomised the quiet luxury of the ludicrously wealthy. He was and always had been utterly beyond her league—even when in old tee and shorts. She should have known it back then but her weak, wanton, wish-driven body had ruled her. She'd succumbed not just to his charm but to her own wildly romantic fantasies. In other words she'd been a complete fool.

She'd been trying to sharpen up ever since. She'd tried for years to push him from her mind but the fact was he'd been there all night tonight. For the first time since she'd left him, she'd gone out with another man. An experiment to see if she even could meet someone else. If she would *ever* want to touch someone else. For over two years she'd kept herself isolated. Certainly not mentioned to her date tonight that she'd been married. Was actually still married. *Separated*. She'd had absolutely no contact with Ares in all that time. Even though they'd not known much detail about him, and what had happened, Elodie and Phoebe had encouraged her to go on a harmless date just to try to help herself get over him because she'd become so *stuck*. She'd done nothing wrong in trying to move forward with her life—indeed she really, deeply, desperately wanted to get over him. But oh, so clearly, she still hadn't. Not that he was *ever* going to know that.

With such long limbs he was able to cover considerable distance with each pace. It was only moments before he was right in front of her. Bethan locked her shaking legs. How could he be more gorgeous than ever? How could his facial structure be even sharper? Her anger ballooned. The man didn't just have pretty privilege, he also had the benefit of a brilliant brain, the advantage of arrogance and, to cap it all off, the supreme rights of the rich. He was unstoppable—*everything* came to him on a platter. *Especially* her.

'Had a nice night, Bethan?' He sounded clipped—coolly controlled—but his glittering gaze homed in on her intensely.

She kept calm through sheer force of will, not letting him see how ferociously he affected her. Still. *Always*. That primal, raw attraction burned to her bones. She couldn't believe the stupidity of her body—didn't she *know* this man?

Oh, yes!

Duh. *More* than in the biblical sense, she knew him for what he truly was—cold-hearted and careless. He was a liar and he used people. She scrambled to recover her wits enough to answer and tried to put her vacuous hormones on ice.

'Ares.' She paused, fleetingly pleased with how steady she sounded. 'I wasn't aware you were in town.'

As if it weren't more than two years since she'd last seen him. Since she'd walked out on their week-old marriage. The whirlwind romance they'd taken too far.

'Obviously not.'

Her anger flared. Did he expect her to be at home pining after him? No matter that she'd been doing exactly that for too long to consider. As if he even cared.

That was the point. He'd never really, truly cared. He'd deceived her. *He* was the one who had cheated. Because it hadn't been a romance for him. It had been a calculated plan that ultimately had nothing to do with her. She'd merely been the tool—the gullible fool who'd believed his seduction meant something.

'Was it a disappointing date?' The edge of his already sculpted jaw sharpened as a muscle tensed. 'You didn't invite him in.'

No. Ares Vasiliadis was the only man she'd ever invited 'in'. But while he knew he'd been her first lover, he didn't need to know he'd still been her *only* lover. He had nothing to do with her any more and had no right to pry into her personal life.

'You were watching me?' she queried coldly.

His mouth compressed.

Her suspicion flared. 'The whole night?'

How was that possible? Why would he have? She was suddenly certain that her prickle of intuition had been bang on but *he* had no right to turn up late at night, unannounced and unexpected. Excitement battled with outrage. Why had he—what was he *thinking*?

She stepped towards him as outrage won and her anger roared. 'It's no business of yours who I spend my time with.'

'No?' He cocked his head and his slow smile was wolfish. 'You think it's not my business?'

'Not at all.' She tensed, knowing she was playing with fire because she recognised that flicker of emotion.

'But of course it is,' he said smoothly. 'You are Bethan Vasiliadis, my errant wife.'

Ares shoved his hands into his pockets not just to hide his fists but to stop himself from grabbing her, pulling her close, pressing her against—

No. He would never do that ever again. Didn't want to. He damned well *did not* want to.

They were done. They'd been done for years. He braced, knowing his was the last face she'd ever wanted to see. He was used to the barely masked loathing in her eyes. It was a look he'd stonily stood before more times than he had dollars in the bank. He drew on the cold rage that had fuelled him since he was thirteen years old and had been the unwanted illegitimate brat forced on his unfaithful father's family, and stayed stock-still. He would remain outwardly unmoved—always—in the face of rejection.

But seeing Bethan in person for the first time in forever—he couldn't stop staring. His pocket Venus. How was she even more beautiful than he remembered? Or was it just that he'd tried so hard *not* to remember that she'd always been a walking fertility symbol with her abundance of curves and softness and pouting lips that were made for him to possess—with his mouth, with his fingers, with his cock. They were filthy, the fantasies that instantly flooded his mind. What he'd do with her and her stunning mouth. Again. Now—

No. He would never do that ever again. Didn't want to. He damned well *did not* want to.

'I never completed the paperwork to take your name,' she said sharply. 'And I'm your *ex*-wife.'

Breathe in for four. Hold for four. Breathe out for four. Hold for four.

Box breathing, the doctor called it, to centre himself, calm the hell down when his pulse raced. Not a heart condition, yet. Just needed to lower the stress levels. Work a little less. Straighten out the kinks. Bethan was definitely a kink. Actually, the impact of her was catastrophic. Apparently she was still his physical weakness, not to mention his biggest mistake. He'd made many mistakes over the years but none like the supreme mess that was the succulent woman before him. He didn't know why *she* did this to him. Why her? Why only ever her? Well, he wasn't succumbing to it this time. Give him twenty-four hours and it would be over. For good.

'Not good with paperwork, are you?' he replied as patronisingly as possible because he knew she hated it. 'Your legal name is indeed Bethan Vasiliadis. And in the eyes of the law you're very much still my wife.'

His AWOL, soon-to-be ex, should have been ex a long time ago…*wife*.

He couldn't hear for the pulse thundering in his ears as for the second time he uttered the word he'd not said in months and he sure as hell couldn't count to four. His wife who'd been out with another man tonight. He gritted his teeth as bitterness burned the back of his throat. He *did not* care.

Bethan's doe eyes widened and her full lips parted. Surely she was not surprised? No way could she still claim to be naïve. Almost two and a half years ago he'd fallen for her sweet routine and while she mightn't be as greedy, she was as untrustworthy as everyone in the 'family' he'd been encumbered with when forced to take the Vasiliadis name himself. She'd bailed the second she could.

'No,' she muttered fiercely.

None of this evening's events should bother him. He should be *pleased* she'd been out on a date. It would make their impending divorce even easier. But he hated it and hated *himself* more for hating it and to stop himself tumbling into a stormy vortex he needed to wrest back control over something. Anything. Ideally *her*.

Yes, that thought hit him satisfyingly hard. Right now he wanted *her* to pay for the hellish evening she'd put him through. For the months—*years*—of hell she'd put him through. For her being as bloody bewitching as ever. But most of all for the fact that she was defying him once more. But Bethan Eagle—Bethan Vasiliadis—wasn't avoiding this moment a minute longer.

His rage had been roiling all day. He'd arrived at her poky flat just as she was walking out of it and into a waiting car. He'd followed on auto. Where was she going, dressed like that? Back when he'd first met her she'd barely worn any make-up but tonight she'd perfectly applied shading to make her eyes sparkle more, her lips even redder. Had that effort been for herself or for someone else? *Someone who wasn't him.*

She'd walked into a restaurant. Ares had had his driver idle so he could see into the window. From the car he'd watched her scan the room, then smile as a man had stood. The jerk couldn't drag his eyes from her as she'd joined him. Two hours of torture had followed as Ares watched and waited. His driver probably thought he was mad. He didn't care. They'd been seated at a table in the front window so the entire date had been visible. He wasn't being a stalker, he merely needed to speak to his ex about completing their damned paperwork. But watching that goodbye scene just now had shot his already sketchy blood pressure through the roof. Her date had clearly wanted to get closer to her. If he'd made a move Ares would have bolted out of the car and done fuck knew what. Not from jealousy. No. But because Bethan had looked flighty as hell. Ares knew her tells but she'd been babbling and so fidgety her discomfort ought to have been obvious to anyone. Fortunately the jerk had given her space—which meant he wasn't a jerk and he'd left at exactly the right time.

Which *wasn't* what Ares would have done. He'd have reached for her. Caged her in his arms. Soothed her anxiety with his hands. Yeah, Ares *was* the jerk here. Always had been. Always would be. He would do whatever it took to get what he wanted—because that was what he'd had to do when he'd been left alone to fend for survival in a family more poisonous than a nest of vipers. But what made him the biggest jerk was that Ares could barely control his 'want' where Bethan was concerned. Her beautiful dress clung to her bountiful curves. Curves that needed a man to handle. They'd been his once. He'd been the first to unwrap her. To taste her. To make her tremble, sigh, scream with pleasure. His stomach churned at the thought of her letting some other guy do that. His old arrogance would have him believe that she never would've sought nor found such pleasure in another man's arms. But he was wrong. Here she'd been, out with someone else and, while she might not have invited that guy in, who knew how many someone elses there had been since he'd seen her last?

'I've not been your wife for years,' she argued, rubbing salt into the wound she'd ripped open.

'I think you'll find the courts might disagree.' He stepped closer.

Satisfaction trickled through him when she didn't back away the way she had from that other guy.

'I'd assumed that, seeing you've not bothered to initiate a divorce, you were happy to remain married to me,' he added.

It had suited him to be unattainable all this time. To thwart the intentions of his unwanted family. And now it suited him to punish her. Just a little. It was nothing on the torture she'd put him through.

Her jaw dropped. 'You thought I was happy?'

Her arrow hit the target. Yeah, that had been his mistake. He *had* thought she'd been happy.

'You were happy in my bed,' he snapped. Because she had been and he needed her to admit at least that small truth.

She froze. It hung between them—the instant rush of unstoppable lust. But that he'd ever be capable of keeping her happy beyond that—that he could ever be enough for her? No. It had been a flight of fancy.

She tore her gaze from his. 'It's only minor paperwork,' she said bravely. 'We had to be separated two years before the divorce can be finalised.'

So she knew that and still hadn't done anything about it.

'You think we've been separated?' He couldn't resist provoking her. 'For these two years and *four months*?' He nearly laughed at the defiant flash in her eyes.

'You haven't accepted that I abandoned you?' Her breath hissed.

Oh, she had. She knew it. He knew it. And the lawyers would certainly agree it was a fact. But right now he would argue the sky was green just to disagree with whatever came out of her beautiful, sultry mouth. He'd missed this—her moving to meet him like a little sparrow taking on a lion. Always game, even when she was way out of her depth and had no chance of winning. That didn't stop her. So once more he steeled himself in readiness for her rejection. Angry that he even had to. But he'd been burned by a young and inexperienced woman. She'd been nobody, had had nothing. He'd given her riches and a lifestyle she'd never known, things he'd not given anyone before. Yet for Bethan it wasn't enough. It had taken a shockingly short time for her to realise she didn't want more than his body—and even that only for a while. Although it seemed that even now she still noticed his physique. He deliberately moved closer, noting the undeniable reaction in her eyes and deepening colour in her cheeks as he entered her personal space.

She didn't back away, but lifted her chin. While he

could appreciate her fiery proud stance in this second, he also hated her for it. He got close enough to feel her heat. It would be nothing to touch her. Kiss her.

No. He would never do that ever again. Didn't want to. He damned well *did not* want to.

'Why haven't you pushed for the divorce, then?' he queried quietly. 'Or is it that you don't really want to?'

Her nostrils flared. 'Of course I want to,' she growled.

'You'd best get to Greece and renounce me, then,' he said huskily, her fury both a reward and an ache.

'I'm never going back to Greece.'

He stared at her appalled expression. Didn't she know? Still a little naïve, then. How sweet. 'But, Bethan, you have to.'

'No, I don't.' A lick of her lip gave her nerves away. 'The lawyers can handle it.'

'Then why haven't you asked them to?'

'Why haven't you?'

His trickle of satisfaction went full flow. He'd come to London to expedite their divorce—as smoothly and easily as possible—because she was right about the time requirement and they were way over it. But she was also very wrong. He would indeed get his damned divorce, but maybe he would also get a soupçon of revenge. Maybe he would make her pay—just a *little*.

Bethan glared up at the man she'd married in a whirlwind few weeks of heady romance. She'd been swept off her feet, consumed by temptation, by the desire to believe the best of him. She'd thought she'd found her fairy-tale romance like the one her parents had. Intense. Wonderful. Easy. Instant. It was laughable what a fool she'd been. But Bethan's childhood home had been filled with photos and her father had shared the stories daily—generous in keeping the memory of her mother alive, in building an impossible ideal. Theirs had been love at first sight and would have lasted a lifetime if her mother hadn't died tragically young.

What was between Bethan and Ares was little more than uncontrolled lust. Always and *only* lust. What she'd naïvely believed was some kind of heroic silent stoicism was Ares coldly forming a calculated plan to use her. Well, she wasn't that dreamy fool now. She was shutting this down and her damned body could hurry up and obey because she'd suffered enough loss already.

But it didn't. Her eyes locked on him, her heart raced, and that traitorous secret part of her melted. It was the *shock*—right? By turning up unexpectedly he'd pitched her headlong into a tumult of conflicting emotions. It wasn't fair of him but then Ares had never played fair. He just did whatever he thought was necessary to get what he wanted, no matter the impact on anyone else. And in only two seconds of being back in his company, she was as attracted as ever. Hormones were such basic things.

'Bethan,' he said slowly as if she were an idiot. 'If you want rid of me as your husband, you have to present in front of the notary. In person. In Greece.'

Uh, *no*. She was never going back to that beautiful place—all steeped in history, in heat and wild herbs and heartache. She'd gone there to honour her grandmother's last wishes, soothing her grief, and met him. She could never, ever go back to the place her already bruised heart had been so brutally broken. But when she didn't answer, his eyebrows lifted superciliously.

'Why hasn't your lawyer informed you of this?'

Because she'd gone to an inexpensive, barely qualified lawyer who'd obviously not had enough experience to tell her. All he'd said was that there had to be a two-year time lag before she could get the divorce. She'd decided to hide out and allow that time to pass. But she hadn't *hidden* all that well. The pitiful truth was a weak part of her had hoped that Ares would come to his senses and come after her. That he would go to the ends of the earth to find her and declare his love in some grand passion...like that fairy-tale, one-and-only romance of her parents. But of course he hadn't because that wasn't what they were. She'd stopped hoping a long time ago and tried to start healing. But the second she saw him tonight, the scab had been ripped off. For a moment—just one stupid moment—she'd thought he was here to get her back. Because she'd taken one look and wanted him as deeply, madly, *badly* again.

'That's why you're here,' she said flatly.

Disappointment thumped all over again. He hadn't had some change of heart and come to see her. He wanted them to be over.

His long lashes dropped, veiling his gleaming eyes. 'Of course, why else?' He cleared his throat and stepped back. 'I see no reason to wait any more. Go inside and get your passport.'

'What?'

'We'll fly to Athens first thing and see the notary in the afternoon.'

Yeah, that didn't explain why she needed to get her

passport right *now*. This commanding attitude was vintage Ares.

'No,' she said slowly—as patronising a tone as he'd used before. 'I'm not flying with you. I'll meet you in court in Athens.'

He folded his arms and shook his head. 'You disappeared on me once already. You think I'll take the risk of that happening again?'

Fire swept through her, pushing her to get in his face. 'Do you really think I'm just going to do whatever you want?' She rose on tiptoe in a vain attempt to get more on eye-level. 'I've wised up, Ares. But you're as controlling as ever. Only out to get what you want.'

'But don't we want the same thing?' He tilted his head, bringing his mouth closer to hers. *'Divorce,'* he enunciated clearly. 'As quickly as possible.' His voice dropped. 'Or is there something else you want?'

'There's *nothing* I want more than to be completely rid of any connection with you.' She jabbed her finger into his chest.

'Nothing you want more?' He grabbed her hand and pressed it flat over his heart.

Stunned, she stilled. She could feel his heart thudding beneath her palm, its pace as fast as her own. And then she felt the fire.

'What are you doing?' She was hot with anger—*not* lust.

'Nothing you want more?' His breath was soft. 'Oh, Bethan, we know that's not the case. That guy could never give you what you need. He's not your type.'

'Don't be feral.' She curled her fingers into a fist, desperate to reject what she was feeling. 'You don't know what I need. Or what my type is.'

'Don't I?' His other arm wound around her waist, holding her in a loose embrace. 'Don't you think I remember exactly what it is you like? How you like it?'

'You think that's you?' She panted, battling the insane urge to lean right against him. 'You're the most arrogant jerk.'

'But am I wrong?' he challenged as if he could feel the yearning tearing her apart. 'I'm the one who taught you, remember?'

Memories flashed. Unstoppable. Unwanted. Undeniable. Their first kiss. Her first time. The way he'd made her shake and scream and in the end cry from the earth-shattering beauty of it. She'd not known what her body was even for until she'd met him. She closed her eyes, trying to block the images flooding her senses. Trying to stop trembling from need. Trying to recover the cold, hard fact that he'd *hurt* her.

Almost no one here in London knew her connection to Ares. She'd reverted to her maiden name, not even told Elodie and Phoebe *who* she'd married or how powerful he was. She'd simply nicknamed him 'the Greek' and she'd been so obviously heartbroken, they'd carefully not pried for details.

She suppressed another tremble. Hating herself for such a damned obvious reaction. She desperately needed to get away and *stay* away from him for good.

'If you don't come with me now, I will contest our divorce and drag it out for years,' he said softly.

'What?' Her eyes flashed open. '*Why* on earth would you do that?'

Didn't he want to be rid of her as quickly as possible too?

'Maybe it's been convenient for me to be married,' he purred, still holding her close.

Oh. Of course. There was the unvarnished truth. Their marriage had always and only been about a convenient benefit for him. It had never been an emotional decision—no love match. But that was what he'd allowed her to believe. And she'd been so infatuated she'd not questioned him as she should have. She'd not stood up for herself and what she deserved. That would never happen again. She was independent and whole. She knew what she wanted. And she would never settle for less ever again. Nor would she ever suffer loss. No more heartbreak. She'd had enough.

'Well, you're not staying married to me,' she snapped. 'We're divorcing and you can't stop it. Go find yourself a new fool.'

'Because you've "wised up"?'

'Absolutely,' she shot back. 'And gotten what I want and need elsewhere.'

'You sure about that?'

His hold on her hadn't tightened any, yet somehow she felt *caged*. Heat overwhelmed her from the inside out. They were barely touching yet they might as well be naked for the fire now scurrying along her veins.

'Let me go,' she breathed. 'Now.'

He immediately dropped his arms and those treacherous cells within her screamed with disappointment. How could she be so weak?

She dragged in a difficult breath. 'I'm not letting you turn my life upside down again.'

'Is that what happened?' he muttered dryly. 'Or was it my life that was wrecked?'

No, *he* didn't get to act as if he'd been at all bothered by her departure.

'I wrecked nothing. You just can't stand that I walked out on you—that the great Ares Vasiliadis was humiliated by the clueless bride he'd thought was infatuated with him. You thought that you could have your cake and eat it too.' She laughed bitterly. 'It's your fault for stringing me along, you know we *never* should have married.'

She wasn't in his league. He didn't just have money, but power and the status of the *elite*. School had taught her how poor outsiders to that level of society fared. Those flush snobs bitchily believed in their superiority. She would never fit in that world—but the worst thing was Ares had known it, he'd planned to *use* that fact.

'So come to Greece,' he said harshly. 'Get this done and then we'll never have to see each other again.'

So he'd not meant that threat to argue against the divorce?

'How long will it take?' she asked.

'You'll only need to be there for the declaration then you can leave again right away.'

One night. Perhaps two. A short stay in an Athens hotel would be expensive but no way was she staying anywhere near him. She'd use the savings she'd been slowly accumulating with her broadening work portfolio but it would be worth it to be free of him at last.

'You want rid of me, right?' he growled.

Desperately. Her awkward date tonight had made it crystal clear. She needed to sever all ties to Ares Vasiliadis. She needed to be free.

'Then come with me now.' He was callous and clearly impatient and his eyes glittered. 'Or are you too scared to spend a mere twenty-four hours with me?'

'Can't you come up with a better tactic than some schoolboy challenge?' she jeered back, then lied through her teeth. 'You don't scare me.'

He shot a disbelieving smile down at her, then bent so his hot whisper brushed the top of her ear. 'I *terrify* you.' He stepped back and sighed, his mouth a thin line. 'Rest assured the feeling's mutual, sweetheart.'

Oh, please. She didn't terrify him, she was nothing more than a minor irritant. But while she'd been putty in his hands over two years ago, she wasn't going to be as malleable this time. The only reason she was considering this was because, in this moment, they wanted the same thing.

'It's really very simple.' He inhaled sharply and braced, legs apart, hands on his hips, every inch a Greek warrior. 'Get your passport. Now. I'm leaving nothing to chance until we're absolutely over.'

CHAPTER TWO

ARES REMAINED TENSE, determined to stay right where he was until she agreed to come with him. It wasn't unreasonable. Naturally he couldn't trust that she wouldn't disappear on him again.

She resisted a few seconds longer then sighed frustratedly. 'Give me five minutes.'

Those five minutes ticked by interminably slowly but he needed every second to recover his self-control. He'd almost hauled her tight against him. Almost kissed her. Almost done everything. In mere moments he'd almost devolved into an out-of-control animal consumed by fury and lust. So quickly she destroyed his humanity.

He counted a breath, reminding himself that he'd already been on the edge having spent those ninety minutes sitting outside that restaurant while she'd flirted with another man. He'd gotten so annoyed he'd knocked back a drink from the car bar. A first. But it had been only the one, so he couldn't blame booze for threatening to fight the divorce. That had slipped out in a moment of pique and Bethan's fury had given him a flicker of perverse pleasure. Shame had swiftly followed. He didn't want to coerce her. That would make him no better than the rest of the Vasiliadis clan—as if his blood carried calculation like poison. The pressure they'd applied on him had been bad enough, but what they'd done to his mother was appalling. Ares had never been able to protect her from the pain they'd inflicted, never been able to right the wrong they'd done her. Nor the wrong *he'd* done her. So he would not do *more* wrong now.

Even though Bethan's body betrayed her, he knew that in truth she wanted to be near him as little as he wanted to be near her. Lust *and* loathing—he understood that complex feeling exactly. But she *did* have to come to Greece. Briefly. Because while they were living apart, the fact remained that without completing that paperwork, if anything happened to him *she* would inherit his entire estate—including the company he'd worked so hard for.

He'd not lied when he'd told her just now that it'd been convenient for him to remain married. Being unavailable meant he thwarted the attempts of the extended Vasiliadis 'family' to control his life and therefore that company. For a while it had amused him to think of his stepmother Gia's panic at the prospect of Bethan gaining all that power. But then the possibility of something *actually* happening to him had hit. No way was he letting Bethan near his work. Not only because she didn't have the experience, but because inheriting a monstrosity was precisely what *had* happened to him. He'd had no idea of the viper's nest he was stepping into when he'd been 'found'—the illegitimate heir of a selfish ass—and forced into a world where he wasn't actually wanted but apparently *needed*. He'd had to survive, not only being thrust into that hell, but that cruellest of evictions from the only home he'd known. He'd done what he'd had to. But it hadn't been enough.

As angry as he was with Bethan on a personal level, he didn't want anything like that happening to her. They'd destroy her in minutes. In one way, they already had. So while he had zero intention of dying any time soon, he needed to devise an alternative succession plan. And he'd long made his point to Gia and the rest of the extended family who coveted the Vasiliadis name. He could never be controlled—would never take the wife they wanted. He would divorce Bethan and then never see her again. Sure as hell never marry again. He couldn't wait.

She finally reappeared from the flat with an overnight bag in her hand. The bastard element within him purred because she'd given in to his demand and that part wanted to demand more. But he would retain his self-control even if it killed him. She climbed into the back of the SUV and fastened her seat belt while he instructed his driver.

'Are we going straight to the airport?' she asked when he settled beside her.

'To a hotel. We'll fly first thing.' He gritted his teeth as she immediately stiffened. 'As awful as I appreciate it will be to spend time with me, this is the fastest way we get what we both want.'

There was a sharp silence.

'Obviously I'll pay for my own room,' she said.

Her prim insistence irritated him all over again. 'On what you earn?'

'How do you know what I earn?'

He couldn't reply immediately. That she'd been willing to work as a *cleaner* to get away from him flicked a deeply personal nerve he couldn't bear to acknowledge.

She swivelled to face him. 'How did you know where I live?'

'I've always known where you are,' he growled.

Her gaze sharpened to a death glare. 'What?'

'Despite the fact you're determined to think the worst of me, I cared enough to be concerned for your well-being. It wouldn't have been a good look if my runaway wife ended up on the streets.'

Her jaw dropped.

'As it was you found a job and a place to live.' He gritted his teeth again.

Her doe eyes widened with anger. 'You've had someone spy on me for all this time?'

'No.' He swallowed. 'I've just been aware of your location and employment status. No details beyond that.'

'Really.' She sounded beyond sceptical.

'Yes,' he snapped. He'd mostly ignored the monthly report he got from the private detective he'd employed to ensure she was okay. He'd known she was thriving. That she'd moved on from cleaning. He'd asked details about her personal life to be omitted. He'd never wanted to know. But it had been shoved in his face tonight. And what had almost happened outside her flat was merely an explosion of that tension. It had been so long since he'd touched a woman. Not that she needed to know that. But unlike her he'd been true to those meaningless vows. Not because he was heroic or pining or anything. He would have, had he been able to perform. Trouble was no other woman had turned him on. And he'd been so bitter by her abandonment, he wasn't about to trust anyone else. Lesson learned, finally. Ares was born to be alone and he desperately needed some other kind of stress release. Because he'd poured himself utterly and totally into his work until his body had had a hissy fit and landed him in hospital for two completely unnecessary days of too many completely unnecessary tests. She didn't need to know about that either.

But it had changed his priorities. What he wanted to accomplish—now he had goals beyond accumulating more billions for the Vasiliadis dynasty. Freeing himself from Bethan was one of them. But her accusing eyes, filling her pale face, ate at the hold on his temper.

'Why would I want to know anything more?' he asked bitterly. 'You walked out on me. You made your feelings abundantly clear.'

She'd left him the first moment she could. Like everyone. But he had himself back under control now and nothing, but nothing, would happen between them again.

'Evidently you didn't want me anywhere near you,' he finished.

Bethan lifted her chin. 'Because evidently you didn't love me. You couldn't even say the words, remember?'

He remembered. He wouldn't, *couldn't*. Her sudden question back then—her *doubt*—had assaulted his own certainty. The words she'd wanted were meaningless. As a boy he'd been told daily that he was loved. That he was wanted. Until one day everything had changed. Words were so easily lies. He wasn't loved nor wanted, but both a burden and an instrument. A weight on two households. Ares would never weaken action with words now.

* * *

Bethan refused to shatter the sharp silence. Despite the gloomy car interior she could see the flash in his eyes and the white ring about his compressed mouth. She'd angered him. Too bad.

'I chase after no one,' he finally said harshly. 'Certainly not a runaway bride.'

Of course he didn't. He'd known where she was all this time and he'd not bothered to make contact because Ares Vasiliadis was a selfish loner who didn't like being backed into a situation he couldn't control. He didn't like being told what to do. Not by anyone.

She'd *thought* he was like her. A hard-working person from a normal background. He'd allowed her to believe it for that first week when they'd met. Until he had her where he wanted her already—in his arms and breathlessly saying yes to everything. She'd been so malleable. So gullible. So easy for him to manipulate. Because he was so used to getting what he wanted— the arrogant and entitled heir of one of the wealthiest families in the world who lived an entirely different existence from hers.

She hadn't known any of that until it was too late— because he'd controlled everything about his situation. He hadn't had the decency to read her in on the reality. He'd let her believe he cared about her. Let her declare her passionate love for him like the naïve lovestruck fool she'd been. She'd trusted and willingly given him all she had. But he hadn't wanted her love. She'd naïvely thought his reticence to talk about his past had been part of their bonding because she too had wounds. But it had been part of his play. She'd seen only what he'd allowed her to see, known only what little he'd been willing to share.

But that trip to Athens after their wedding had revealed things he'd wanted to conceal for longer. He'd told her they were going to finalise paperwork, make arrangements for her new bank cards and the like. She'd been desperately nervous arriving at his family 'compound'—the word alone setting off alarm bells. It had been *enormous*. Super formal and cold. Which was exactly how Ares had turned the second he stepped across the threshold.

Too late she'd discovered he had no intention of bringing her fully into his life. It was only thanks to a passing comment from his stepmother, Gia, followed by a frantic Internet translation of the Greek social pages, that she'd discovered that he'd long been meant to marry someone else. Apparently the engagement between Ares Vasiliadis and Sophia Dimou was finally imminent. The numerous photos of his prospective fiancée had triggered every insecurity Bethan had. The woman was beautiful, wealthy, accomplished, perfectly *appropriate*. Gia's words had whipped open the scars left by schoolgirl bullies and caused far deeper wounds. It had been unfathomable to Bethan—and of course the rest of the world—why Ares had opted to marry *her* in such a hasty, impulsive rush instead. So she'd actually grown some courage and asked him. That was when she'd discovered how impervious he was to anyone else's feelings. He'd already gone quiet and self-contained. In that instant he'd turned to ice.

He hadn't denied the engagement rumours, just dismissed them as irrelevant. Then he'd made her feel even more inferior by coolly informing her that she wouldn't have to come to Athens much if *she* found it too stressful...

But Athens was where *he* worked. Where his family was. The family she'd hoped to fit into. She'd realised he was *ashamed* of her—that he didn't want her with him when he was around those people. He'd gone so remote. When she'd asked if he loved her, he'd not even bothered to answer.

She'd been so heartbroken she couldn't stay. Insecure and desperate, she'd run. And he'd let her. So much for her love story for the ages—the whole thing had been too good to be true. He'd betrayed her trust and broken her dreams and Bethan absolutely *hated* him.

But at least now he wanted their marriage to be over and she could hardly be hurt more when she wanted the same. Except the soul-destroying truth was she still was physically attracted to him while that last part of her romantic self still ached for the idyllic 'big family dream' she'd woven around him. Her childhood home had been a safe shelter from the misery at school. Her grandmother had loved her, spent hours teaching her traditional skills, telling her stories of her parents, of her own relationship, until she'd become ill. Her father had spent what time he had ashore teaching her everything *he* could too and it was wonderful. But he had been posted away more often than not. So while she'd been loved, she'd been lonely.

She'd longed for a husband who loved her and children—wanting them to have the siblings she'd not had. She'd planned a life filled with people and joy because there *had* been joy at home until she'd lost them both.

She'd just wanted *more*. For five minutes she'd thought she could build that with Ares. But she'd not indulged in that foolish fantasy at all in the time since she'd left him. She'd focused on building an independent life for herself. She didn't want or need a partner. Her career was fulfilling—creative and growing. She was proud of what she'd achieved and her girlfriends provided the safe, supportive emotional haven she'd missed.

But right now Elodie was away and Phoebe was coping with an unplanned pregnancy and heartbreak. She *hadn't* been up waiting for Bethan tonight. Bethan had figured she'd gone to bed early, so had left her a quick note explaining she'd be away for a couple of days and not to worry—certainly not mentioned 'the Greek'. She would talk to them about him fully when she got back. Hopefully she'd be able to because this would be truly over.

She ignored him the rest of the brief drive. She wasn't going to attempt small talk—there was no need to fill the silence. She'd learned to control her nervous babbling. Mostly. The only thing to focus on was that this could be over quickly and with minimal impact. She *was* different. Wiser, more confident. She wouldn't let Ares walk all over her again. It was only a few hours to endure. She would go to Greece, secure the end of their mockery of a marriage and finally be free.

The driver turned into the hotel drop-off zone. It was predictably luxurious. Naturally his sumptuous penthouse suite had a stunning view. Without a word she marched straight into the bedroom that was clearly uninhabited and locked the door.

She showered. Got into bed. Tried to relax. Fell asleep

for five minutes before waking—heart racing—from a steamy dream. She tossed, turned, tangled in the top sheet until, too plagued by memories, she abandoned the idea of sleep altogether. Something ice cold might settle her furnace of a body. By now Ares would surely be asleep so she could grab something from the bar in the lounge. She was halfway across the room when she spotted him silently watching her from the sofa near the window.

'Are you seriously keeping guard because you think I'm going to sneak out in the middle of the night?' she jeered furiously.

'No.' He shot her a withering glance. 'I'm working.'

Shirtless. On the sofa. With his laptop on the low table in front of him. Bethan's inner furnace was on full meltdown.

His gaze narrowing, he stood and stepped towards her. 'What's wrong?'

She gaped at his half-naked body. Failed to drag her eyes away. Just as she'd always failed. He was even more perfect—muscled, lean, bronzed.

'What do you need?' he prompted huskily.

'I was thirsty,' she mumbled, backing away. 'But it doesn't matter.'

He veered away from her. For another second Bethan still stared—taking in the way his broad back tapered to slim hips and tight butt. Blinking, she stormed back to her room.

A minute later he knocked. 'Bethan.'

No ignoring that imperious tone. Gritting her teeth, she reopened the door. Keeping his distance, he held a small bottle towards her. She noted its elegant shape and pretty label and died inside.

Do not look up. Do not wonder what the expression is in his eyes.

Because this *wasn't* deliberate or meaningful. Yet every muscle weakened.

'Thanks.' She reached out, mentally cursing her trembling fingers.

As soon as she got it, she shut the door, turning to rest her spineless self against the wood. She gazed at the bottle, unsure she could stomach the memories a taste from it would invoke. But she was unbearably thirsty and desperately tempted because she loved this and it had been *so* long. She unscrewed the cap, sipped and sure enough was instantly transported back to the day she'd met him…

Barely dawn, the day was already scorching. Bethan slowly strolled from her hostel to find the ferry to take her to Avra, the small island she'd heard was a 'must-visit' but difficult to reach. The harbour was still, there were only a couple of boats by the jetty and only one broad-shouldered man hunched down by the ropes of one.

'Excuse me, is this the ferry to Avra?'

He glanced up briefly, blinked, then rose to his full height to stare down at her. For forty seconds she just stared back at the most handsome man she'd ever seen. When he finally cocked his head and quirked an eyebrow, she awkwardly remembered herself, stammered a repeat of the question before nerves made her babble a fast and incoherent explanation he didn't need and quite possibly didn't even understand. She twisted the bangle on her wrist, heat filling her face until he finally glanced at his watch and she fell silent.

'We will leave shortly,' he muttered.

She blinked. 'Really? Are you sure?'

He turned his back to release the rope. Not wanting to miss the ride, she stepped aboard. Her pulse didn't settle and her brain ceased to function. She just stared. His grey tee shirt was worn and hugged his shoulders, the linen shorts looked equally old and soft but everything visible above and below was perfection—long limbs, fine muscles, and the most beautiful blue-grey eyes she'd ever seen. Desperately she sipped the last of the water from her small plastic drink bottle, melting from not just the heat but the vision before her.

She was unable to stop herself staring at the grumpy Greek god for the entire crossing. He knew of course. She was hardly surreptitious. Every so often he'd glance back at her. But there was no smile, no break in the grumpy demeanour. He was silent the whole time and she was too bowled away by his looks to think properly. So she didn't compute that it wasn't a huge ferry, that he'd not asked her for payment nor that there were no other passengers. She was just...utterly brainless.

When they finally arrived she jumped ashore to catch the mooring line and secure it to the cleat on the dock. She caught surprise in his eyes but then he looked her up and down and made her feel more self-conscious. She caught her breath as he stepped close. He took the empty water bottle from her limp fingers, then moved to the back of the boat while she dragged in a recovery breath. He returned only a few moments later and handed back her bottle—refilled with fresh water. He then put a wide-brimmed hat on her head. Stunned, she didn't know what to say.

'The village is tiny,' he said in accented, but perfect English and her body responded as if it were the sexiest thing it had ever heard.

'There's no transport,' he added. 'So you have to follow the path, walk up the hill.'

She swore she saw doubt in his eyes and defensiveness flared. She might be curvy and a bit limp in the heat, but she would be fine. 'I'm fit enough.'

His sensuous mouth curved. 'I'm very aware how fit you are.'

It was the lightest flirtation but she blushed madly and almost tripped over her own feet. A full smile broke on his face—a beam of genuine amusement that utterly bowled her over. She fell—intensely and irrevocably. But they'd docked and presumably he needed to depart and she'd been a dork already so she stammered her thanks and started her slow trek up the narrow path to the village, refusing to turn back for another look at him. She'd embarrassed herself enough.

It took her more than twenty minutes to get to the top. The first thing she saw was a small taverna with a stunning view of the sea below. At that early hour there was only the one customer seated at one of the tables outside. A man. Bethan stopped. Stared. Two bottles were in front of him. How had he gotten there ahead of her? But he flashed that tantalising smile and she was sunk.

'Need something refreshing?' He jerked his chin towards the bottles. 'Try this.'

At the cool amusement in his eyes, the challenge,

something flared within. Bethan, who'd been shy and withdrawn for so long, refused to run away from this.

She unscrewed the cap of the elegant glass bottle and sipped the lemonada—*infused with a particular tree extract, native to only one Greek island, it had zing and a distinctly different aroma. It was deliciously refreshing.*

'That wasn't the ferry, was it?' She eventually smiled at him. 'And you're not a ferryman.'

'How'd you work it out?' His smile flickered.

'You didn't ask for payment.'

He met her gaze directly. 'Maybe I'm asking now.'

'What's it going to cost me?'

'A little of your time...'

CHAPTER THREE

ARES BARELY SLEPT, tormented by memories of the day they'd met. Her ridiculous, endearing assumption that he was the ferryman; the naïveté with which she'd readily stepped aboard his outboard. She'd been an absolute innocent abroad with a guileless belief in the goodness of others meaning she seemingly had no consideration for her own personal safety. He'd said yes to protect her from the less honourable assholes who would flock given half the chance.

He scoffed at his self-indulgent pretence. *He'd* been the predator. He'd taken one look and wanted her and by the time he'd gotten her across the water—aware not only of her gaze on him, but of her unfettered appreciation of the sun and sea—he'd been ruthlessly determined. Then he'd discovered she really had been an innocent. A virgin of all things and on her first overseas trip. He'd enjoyed educating her in the beauty of Greece and the heat of the bedroom. Her enthusiasm had been intoxicating, the pleasure of her so heady he'd actually thought her a stunningly novel solution to the relentless pressure of the family he loathed. She'd been sweet, so easy to please, he'd thought their arrangement would be perfect. Massive mistake. Because she'd met that family, listened to their poison and the fantasy had ended within hours.

He hated thinking of that moment. Their betrayal, he'd expected. Hers, he'd not. Now they sat side by side in the car again, physically close yet more distant than ever. She was dressed in black trousers and a black blazer, he could see a black tee beneath. Covering up with the most businesslike attire he'd ever seen her in. If her intention was to maintain professional distance and keep them on a cool footing, it wasn't working. She looked more desirable than ever.

Fifty minutes later he led her across the tarmac. She stared at the plane with a bitter expression.

'Figures,' she muttered scathingly.

Yeah, she'd only been in the boat and the helicopter. Not his jet. For reasons he still didn't understand, Bethan genuinely wasn't interested in his wealth. Something that had made her amusingly unique in his world. He watched her board ahead of him. Her loose hair gleamed in the morning sun—such a rich brunette—as luxuriant and abundant as the rest of her. But her face was pale, shadows clung beneath her brown eyes as if she'd not had a deeply restful night. She sat in one of the large chairs and immediately pulled something from the side pocket of her overnight bag. Knitting needles. Of course. Now he remembered how her pretty, dexterous fingers were rarely still. In those days together she'd always been working on something—when he hadn't been distracting her and helping her discover how phenomenally good she was with her hands in other ways… She would poke him in the eye with the needle if he tried to 'distract' her now.

She'd told him she'd learned knitting and other crafts from her grandmother. She'd lived with her while her father was at sea. A navy man who'd taught her every knot as well as how to navigate, how to handle a wheel... Her love of the water was in her blood, as it was his.

'Were the needles your grandmother's?' He couldn't resist asking.

'Yes.' She didn't take her eyes off the wool as she replied. 'They're more precious to me than anything.'

Certainly more precious than the rings he'd given her and was no longer wearing.

He fidgeted uncomfortably. Love of the sea wasn't the only thing they'd had in common. Like him she had no siblings—well, not quite like him. He'd had a half-brother—Alex—who'd died before they'd had a chance to meet. Though of course, had Alex lived, Ares likely never would have met him and his life would have been drastically different. But as it was both Alex and their father, Loukas, had died. Ares had been brought in—forcibly installed as usurper.

He'd wanted escape from all that for just a little while. So for a few days he'd explored the local bays with Bethan on his small outboard until he'd finally confessed that he owned a fleet of ships. She'd not believed him initially. That was when he'd taken her to the villa. She'd declared it paradise, the one place she never, ever wanted to leave. Tensely, he shoved that unhelpful recollection away and watched her nimble fingers. She didn't snatch glances the way she had the day they'd met. Today she was fully in control and focused on her task—whereas he'd been too distracted to hold a razor steady this morning and couldn't stop staring now.

Rubbing the stubble on his jaw, he sank deeper into his seat and surrendered to the overpowering need to just watch her. The pattern was intricate. She was multitalented, any kind of craft she could master immediately. It was more than skill and practice, it was a gift. And he couldn't bring himself to interrupt her even though they had business to attend to.

She had the fullest of mouths, the lushest of curves—her breasts were so much more than a handful and, yeah, he was *appalling* because his palms itched now.

Rock hard, he shifted awkwardly and lifted his gaze—trying to block memory and temptation—and was instantly fascinated by the fierce concentration in her deep brown eyes.

It wasn't until they landed that he even remembered he'd intended to discuss the settlement details with her—he was rendered *that* useless. She was dressed for business. Maybe that was how *he* had to treat this. He would take her to the office and finalise everything there. Then he'd install her in a hotel room, stick a guard on her door and ensure she didn't leave without seeing the notary tomorrow.

Bethan carefully packed away her precious needles and knitting she'd spent the entire flight working on, but the truth was she'd screwed up the pattern so badly she was going to have to start over entirely. The little blanket she was making for Phoebe's baby was so full of holes it looked as if a swarm of moths had been at it. Her grandmother would tease her mercilessly if she were alive to see it. But Bethan had been far too aware of Ares. She didn't know why he'd spent the entire flight wordlessly watching her but she wasn't about to ask.

She stepped out of the plane, felt the heat—and hit—of memory. Athens had been the scene of her total devastation. Blinking away that rising emotion, she walked to the sleek car. The waiting driver didn't meet her gaze, doubtless drilled in discretion. Unwilling to betray her nerves, she didn't ask Ares where they were going but it didn't take long to figure out.

The Vasiliadis company headquarters were in the heart of Athens' business district. The stunning architecturally designed building echoed the body of a ship, reflecting the nature of the family interests. Multi-storeyed, with a water feature and an emerald lawn on one of the upper balconies, it exemplified luxury, infinite resources and glamour. Just like Ares himself and of course those magnificent boats in his luxury yacht division. As for the merchant marine side, that was pure economic efficiency and excellence.

Stiffly she accompanied him into the vast building. The receptionist tried to speak as they swept past but Ares snapped something short, immediately silencing the poor man. Bethan gritted her teeth more tightly. The gleaming elevator had no buttons. Apparently it simply recognised the supremely important occupant and immediately swept them up to the right floor.

'Are the lawyers meeting us here?' she asked as soon as they were alone in the spacious statement office—white and blue with unimpeded views in every direction. She'd only been in it once before.

'Tomorrow,' he said brusquely. 'I've engaged an independent one for you.'

'I don't need—'

'The court documents are in Greek,' he interrupted tersely. 'So you will have an independent translator as well.' He rubbed the back of his neck. 'You can trust I have your best interests at heart.'

'I don't need you to have my best interests at heart.'

He lifted an envelope marked private from the large desk and passed it to her. 'Here. Read it.'

Taking it, she moved away to scan the first few pages that were, thankfully, in English, mentally appreciating her superstar admin-queen friend, Phoebe, for showing her how to read legal jargon in the sale and purchase contracts for the props supplies she'd ordered. This contract had some appalling parallels. She shuffled through the sheets of paper, aghast at their utterly offensive contents, before lifting her head to glare at him. 'This is a divorce *settlement*. I don't need a settlement.'

'No?' He met her accusing stare coolly. 'You don't want to milk me for my money?'

She wasn't in the mood for joking. She'd been stuck on that plane in too close proximity to him for hours and she needed this to be over. *Now*.

She tossed the pages on the table and paced further away from him. 'I don't need your money or anything else.'

'It's been drawn up for months,' he retorted. 'I'm not a complete jerk, Bethan. I was never going to leave you destitute.'

'I'm not destitute. I'm doing just fine.' She turned back, daring him to tell her that what she earned wasn't enough.

He thought he knew everything but he *didn't*. Yes, she'd started as a cleaner for the escape rooms Elodie managed, but Elodie had caught her repairing one of the props and invited her to work on them. She'd swiftly graduated from prop maintenance to creation. When a theatre director who'd visited the escape rooms had asked Elodie where she got her props from, she'd introduced him to Bethan. She'd then submitted samples for his next production and he'd contracted her for them and more. Her name was becoming known in theatre circles for bespoke items.

But her most precious success had been with the multi-media pieces she made for her own creative expression and joy. She had enough time, after all, to explore all the craft and trade skills she'd acquired and she'd studied more. Last year Phoebe had encouraged her to enter one into an art auction and to her amazement it had sold. Bethan had suspected that Phoebe and Elodie had clubbed together to buy it but they'd insisted that wasn't the case. According to the auctioneer a business had bought it to put in their reception area. Bethan had been delighted and inspired to keep working on those one-off pieces. People believed they were art and maybe one day she'd hold her own exhibition. That one major success had instilled belief in her. It was one dream that might actually be possible.

Ares didn't answer or argue—he simply bypassed her, strolling to the corner of his office. A moment later he turned back holding a platter that someone must have delivered in the few minutes before they'd arrived. His staff were impeccably trained and basically invisible with it. He set it on the low coffee table. Bethan recognised several of the meze dishes—each was associated with a memory she couldn't cope with right now. She told her mouth not to water, but the first time she'd eaten melitzanosalata was the afternoon they'd first kissed and he'd fed her stuffed cucumber cups in the beach hut when she'd needed cooling down after a particularly vigorous encounter. Her heat rose, as did her heart rate. And with it, panic. She couldn't think about this. Couldn't be alone with him any more.

'Let's take a moment and refuel,' he broke into her thoughts gruffly. 'Then we'll talk this through rationally.'

'There's nothing to talk through.' She didn't need to be treated like a child and she couldn't stand to be near him.

A muscle in his jaw ticced and he stepped towards her. 'You need to eat something. You barely ate dinner last night, didn't bother with breakfast and hardly touched lunch on the flight.'

Her skin tightened, stilling her. 'How do you know I barely ate dinner?'

His gaze dropped from hers to the platter.

'Were you there for that entire date?' Aghast, she moved towards him. 'Did you watch me *all* that time?'

She'd known he'd followed her but surely it hadn't been for that long?

Ares didn't meet her eyes but she knew guilt when she saw it. 'Ares?'

'It was hardly a fantastic date, was it?' he snapped sarcastically. 'You pushed food round the plate and escaped without a single touch. I needed to talk to you, seeing you are still my wife and all.' He stepped towards her. 'At least be grateful I didn't interrupt that stilted conversation and embarrass you more. Had you told him about me?'

'There was no need, given you're not part of my life,' she threw back. 'And I can go on as many dates with as many men as I want.'

She saw his anger spark, but hers was already ablaze and she wasn't about to back down. She was utterly humiliated that he'd seen how awkward that date was. It was none of his business and she was never telling him it had been her first date in for ever. 'As if you've been single this whole time—'

'Oh, but of course I have,' he cut her off bitterly. 'Unlike you, I've honoured the promises I made when we married.'

She gaped. He was lying. He *had* to be lying. Ares Vasiliadis lied to make himself look good. He had no compunction about it. He'd thrown that out just to make her feel bad. Which she refused to do because she *hadn't* been unfaithful. She hadn't kissed anyone and certainly not slept with anyone either before or since him. But that was irrelevant, she was free to date because they were *separated*. She hadn't seen him for more than two years—not since the day he'd refused to tell her he loved her. Because he didn't. So she owed him nothing and he had no right whatsoever to judge her behaviour. Yes, she was worked up, and weak and unable to resist and she couldn't resist clarifying—giving him the chance to come clean—because she desperately still wanted to know whether there was any spark of truth in that statement.

'You're saying you've been celibate since I left.' She swallowed, her throat tight and sore.

She was prepared for silence. He didn't like to answer personal questions.

His stormy gaze didn't leave hers. 'Yes.'

The world fell away from her feet. 'I don't believe you.'

He walked slowly towards her. 'When did I ever lie to you, Bethan?'

Anger coloured everything red. She welcomed it—better that than any other emotion that surged in his presence. 'I told you, I'm not the naïve fool I was back then.'

'*When* did I lie?' he repeated harshly—a breath away from her now.

In those exact vows he'd just referred to—when he'd promised to love her! A word he'd *refused* to use before or after the damned wedding ceremony they'd had on the beach barely two weeks after they'd met.

But now he stood toe-to-toe with her.

'*You* lied to *me*,' he said softly. 'You didn't trust me. You left me. *Not* the other way round, Bethan.'

She tensed. She *had* left—and with good reason. Because omission could also be a lie. But if that was the narrative he needed to get through this, so be it. She would let him have some moral high ground. She was too angry to care. What *she* really needed was to get the hell away from him because she wasn't going to lose herself in lust—in wanting him more than her next breath—again. Yet her body rebelled—total traitor to her reason—defying her mental will and following basic instinct. Her body knew this man gave pleasure. It was imprinted on every cell and it had been so long that she was almost quaking with need. But he could never know that. This time at least she would keep *some* boundaries. Some dignity.

'Just give me the damned divorce, Ares.' She choked out. 'I don't need—'

'Anything else from me,' he finished for her in a rough growl. 'I've got that.' He moved closer, emotion streaming from him. 'But what about *want*?'

He was an inch from her and she knew that look in his eyes and her treacherous body revelled in its power. Ares was unleashed—all emotion and the only emotion *he* knew was lust. She named it, because this she knew he couldn't deny—not even wordlessly. She wouldn't let him. Not now. '*You* want *me*.'

His eyes—more grey than blue—burned through her. He'd reverted to that serious, grumpy, intense man she'd met that hot morning in Greece. 'Always. Because I am *damned*.'

Fierce pleasure exploded within her at his husky admission—more when he swept her close. *Honesty* at last. But all that mattered was that his mouth was on hers again. She strained up—kissing him back—and his arms tightened, lifting her off her feet. She shivered, a violent ripple of yearning and relief. *This* she needed. This she'd *missed*.

He lowered her back to the floor and bent closer—big and ravenous. Pressing kisses down her neck, he shoved her blazer from her shoulders. She shook it free and tunnelled her fingers through his hair—holding him to her. Their lips locked again, tongues swept and delved. Damned? It had been so damned long and it was so damned good. He pushed her tee up her body, exposing her bra to his burning gaze. His hands cupped her, thumbs trailing up the crest of her bra to where her breasts spilled over the lacy edge. His growl was pure animal and he took her taut nipple into his hot mouth. Heat shot from her breasts to her lower belly and her hips swirled, pressing against the hardness of his. His hands moved faster, heavy and sure. He slid fingers beneath her waistband, straight into her panties. She quivered as he boldly stroked between her legs.

'*Damn*, Bethan.' He raised his head and stared right into her eyes, adding a muffled mutter of something hot and filthy.

'Touch me,' she growled. Not just willing and wanton. *Demanding.*

She wasn't the innocent who'd let him do anything any more, she was the woman who would push for what she needed from him.

Next moment he'd swept her trousers and panties to her ankles and perched her on the edge of the sofa. And then he was there. On his knees, his hands holding her firmly so he could kiss her—hot and intimate. With every lush nibble, stroke and lick she arched—closer and closer. She moaned, bucking beneath the tormenting erotic touches. He reached up and pressed a hand across her mouth—half silencing her moans—but she took the chance to tease the centre of his palm with her tongue. She needed part of him to kiss.

He growled and nuzzled closer, eating her, fingering where she was hot and wet and hungry. His other hand muffled her scream. Caught in ecstasy, she clutched his hair, her hips writhing, pressing him closer to her.

Not that she needed to because his suction on her was total and his hold on her hard. Neither of them relinquished the other even through her violently intense orgasm. But when she finally went limp, he pulled away. She panted, gazing up at him as he then braced both his fists either side of her body, pressing into the arm of the sofa. Not touching her. His muscles rippled with the effort of restraint but she didn't understand why he was now holding back.

'Ares?' she muttered, confused.

He shook his head. Pre-empting her plea. Rejecting her already.

She gritted her teeth. Desperately stopping herself from repeating his name. From *begging*. She dropped her gaze. She wouldn't let him see he'd just destroyed her. Again. Not with that orgasm, but by not giving her all of himself when she'd given him all of her. He'd given her pleasure. He'd made her lose control. But he hadn't given her the trust of letting himself go in her arms and body. He'd held back—his body this time, his heart *always*. And it hurt.

'We can't, Bethan,' he ground out. 'I don't have protection with me and I'm sure the last thing you want is my baby.'

She flinched as he pushed away and stalked across the room, tucking his shirt back into his trousers while she remained sprawled and stunned.

Once upon a time she'd wanted his baby more than anything. She'd been so naïve. Back then he'd skimmed over that discussion, merely mentioning in passing that she and any children would have a wonderful life on Avra. That crumb had been enough for her to envisage a glorious future—her fantastical imagination had grown an entire paradise from that tiny seed. Now humiliation burned. She quickly fixed her trousers and tee and swept up her blazer.

'That shouldn't have happened.' He ruffled his hand through his hair, leaving it no less spiky.

No kidding. Honestly, she wasn't even sure how it had. But there was a small balm in the fact he was still breathless.

As was she. One moment they'd been arguing, the next they'd exploded into a tawdry encounter in his office. His door hadn't even been locked and she'd ended up half naked on his sofa—exposed for anyone to see had they walked in. Shame poured through her. She was so *weak*. Brushing her hair behind her ear, she tried to release the remnants of that bliss to understand what had just happened. *Why* had he made her come but not lost control himself? Had he wanted to exert his sensual power over her? Well, he'd succeeded. She'd given into it—him—so easily. Angry energy fired through her system because she knew he'd *wanted* her too. She'd heard his groans. She'd felt the hard ridge of his reaction. He'd ravished her like a starving man... Only to reject her when she was at the point of absolute surrender.

She turned her back and closed her eyes against the stinging tears. She needed to toughen up. She'd equated hot sex with heartfelt emotion before. Lust with love. She'd thought his inability to keep his hands off her had meant something *more*. She knew better now. And she really needed to leave.

She cleared her throat and hauled herself together. 'Please summon a driver. I'd like to go to my hotel.'

In the ensuing moment of silence regret swamped again, a wave of futile longing that things could've been different—had he *loved* her. But he'd only wanted her and, even then, not enough.

'We'll meet with the lawyers tomorrow,' he answered tightly. 'Don't worry, you don't have to be alone with me again.'

Her humiliation was complete. They both knew that she'd wanted *more*—more than he had. Again.

'I'll escort you to the car.'

She really didn't want him to do that, but as she couldn't figure her way out of the too-high-tech building she had little choice. She stood stiff and silent beside him at the back of the elevator, staring straight ahead. She refused to cry or tremble but she'd never felt as empty or as alone and she'd never ached this much. In all this time, there'd not been a moment as bad as this.

'Bethan.'

She closed her eyes, blocking his damned intense whisper. She didn't want to hear anything he had to say. But then his fingers stroked her jaw, coaxing her with all the tenderness she'd needed after such an explicit, raw encounter. But it was *too late*.

'Look at me,' he breathed.

Her eyelashes fluttered of their own volition. His fingers gently nudged—turning her face. As she fully opened her eyes she saw he'd turned to face her. She stilled, surprised by the regret blooming in *his* eyes. His cheeks flushed as something else that she couldn't—*shouldn't*—figure out deepened in his expression. Something intimate and exposed.

'Bethan—'

Upbeat music suddenly intruded on their burgeoning intimacy. But there was no music in this too smooth elevator. Bethan heard a gasp but Ares's sensuous lips were still pressed together. She turned her head and saw the elevator doors had opened. But they weren't at the basement garage level, they were on another floor and there were people—so *many* people staring in at them.

'Ares,' Bethan hissed, wildly casting about for a button to close the doors but the lift was so modern you needed the blasted right biometrics to get it to do anything and she didn't have them. 'Ares, close the door.'

He finally turned from her. In a blink he took in the open elevator doors and the staring throng, grasped her arm and drew her forward with him, a wide smile pinned to his arrogant face.

'Good afternoon, everyone.'

His transformation was instant and total—from intense and stormy to cool but polite. He propelled her so forcefully that she was almost lifted off the ground as he swept them into the hyenas' den. It happened so fast she had no time to resist.

'Five minutes,' he muttered beneath his breath.

He couldn't possibly be serious. She had stubble rash between her thighs. Her mouth was swollen from the roughness of those kisses, she was sure her face was flushed and she could hardly breathe, let alone figure out what to do. But one fact cut through her shattered emotions. Ares was *utterly* controlled in this moment. *He* looked utterly unaffected—as if those moments in his office—when his mask had dropped—had never happened. How could he *possibly* be calm right now? His remote demeanour was so unfathomable that an outlandish suspicion occurred to her—had he stopped the elevator on this floor *deliberately*?

Already beyond stressed in the last twenty-four hours, she now felt anger unlike any other brew within her. But there were too many people around to cause more of a scene. She had no idea why there were at least sixty people present, all in sharp cocktail attire. It had to be a celebration—perhaps of their latest billion? Another massive boat deal? But whatever it was, they didn't give a damn about it now because whispers rippled the length of the impeccably decorated room. She didn't need to speak the language to understand, she *saw* the wide-eyed speculation and knew several clearly recognised her. She'd walked into a hostile environment and faced whispers and condescension like this before. The flashing memory of high-school bullies didn't hurt today, indeed she could almost appreciate that relentless, horrible experience because it meant she *almost* didn't care about these people doing the same now. She was only interested in understanding the enigma that was Ares. If he'd done this deliberately, *why*? What was he playing at?

But she couldn't ask, he'd already been collared by two tall, loud men who were quickly telling him something terribly serious-sounding in Greek. In a second he'd effortlessly slipped into the CEO persona she'd never really seen in action before.

Keeping her head high, she lifted a glass of champagne from the tray a waiter offered, but downed it too quickly as she walked further into the crowded reception room, fuelling the angry fire she needed to face so many curious, judgemental stares. And suddenly it wasn't only anger hurtling through her, but jealousy too.

Sophia Dimou stood ten feet away. The woman Ares was meant to have married was everything Bethan wasn't. Tall, willowy and from a family already connected to the fine and mighty Vasiliadis dynasty. When Ares had turned up in Athens after a two-week break with Bethan as his bride, shock waves had shuddered through the city and beyond.

Bethan had tried not to care about the opinions of those strangers, but she'd *desperately* yearned to be welcomed into his *family*. Because her family were the ones who'd held her close and made her feel safe. She'd ached to find that same from Ares's family, given her own were gone. So she'd wanted to make a good impression. But she'd had no idea what they were like and Ares hadn't warned her. They were *cold* and haughty. And perfect.

Gia Vasiliadis, Ares's stepmother, approached her now. Beautiful, powerful, utterly intimidating. Just over two years ago Bethan hadn't just been apprehensive, she'd also been a push-over. Too eager to please, too earnest in her attempt to fit in. So she'd listened to *everything* Gia had said. This time, she wasn't going to be as easily affected. She wouldn't let this woman *matter*.

'I didn't realise you and Ares were still so in *touch*.' Gia unsubtly emphasised that last.

Bethan knew it looked as if they'd been intimate in the elevator and it had to be obvious she'd been kissed to within an inch of her life, given her mouth was throbbing with the bruising from the passionate kisses she was no longer used to. And Ares had that arrogant aura of a man who'd gotten what he wanted. So there was no point in trying to deny anything. Besides, the malicious tone in Gia's question set Bethan's teeth on edge. She'd lost everything here once before. She would keep her dignity this time.

'Ares and I prefer to keep our relationship private,' she answered softly.

'You call that private?' The man who'd accompanied Gia smirked.

Dion was Ares's father's cousin. Now Gia's partner. They did like to keep things in the family here—given Sophia Dimou was Gia's niece.

'You're back together?' Gia asked before Bethan could comment on his quip.

Bethan allowed a Mona Lisa smile to curve her lips. She wouldn't be that naïve girl who was too open with these people again. That had made her too vulnerable. She wouldn't give Gia or Dion anything to hurt her this time.

'You're not wearing your rings.' Gia frowned.

'They're at the jewellers. The diamond setting needed tightening and it was an opportunity to have both cleaned.' Bethan tried to sound calm even as she babbled.

Sophia stepped closer—unashamedly listening. As she lifted her glass to her mouth, Bethan saw the huge emerald adorning her finger. It was definitely an engagement ring. Bethan's jealousy sharpened. Was *this* why Ares wanted to finalise the divorce now? Had he finally proposed to Sophia as he should have years ago? She was horrified. 'I—'

'Bethan was just telling us about your relationship,' Gia interrupted loudly. 'I didn't know you were back together, Ares. That's a surprise.'

Ares's heavy arm landed along Bethan's shoulders and squeezed her close. Chagrined, Bethan stared at Gia. She hadn't said they were back together—she hadn't actually answered! She looked down into her empty glass. Ares had been right. She should have eaten more today. She might have made better decisions.

'Oh?' Ares queried coolly.

Bethan tilted her head back to meet his eyes and didn't deny it. What was the point in contradicting Gia now? She saw fury flare before he damped it down— back to that calm, arrogant, smooth man in a heartbeat. She blinked. He was so *very* good at masking his true emotions in public. She'd just seen it twice in the space of twenty minutes. Masking lust. Masking fury. Those were strong emotions, so he was well practised. Now, at the worst time, for the *first* time, she wondered why and how he'd become quite so good at it. Why had he never warned her about his family? Why was he now as cold and as remote as he'd turned when they'd finally been alone again after meeting his aunt, that moment when Bethan had asked if he even loved her? And now his stormy grey gaze met hers briefly then his grip on her tightened and he pulled her right against his taut body, stopping her from thinking at all.

'What makes you think we were ever apart?' he drawled.

Gia's and Dion's jaws dropped simultaneously. Another round of whispers rippled around the room, worse, from the corner of her eye Bethan saw a couple of people actually had their phones out. Were they *filming*?

'Just because we live in separate countries doesn't mean we're actually separated,' Ares added quite audibly.

Why was he saying this? Why go along with such an outrageous fiction? But his hold on her was too strong to escape and suddenly she remembered the threat he'd made to her yesterday.

'Bethan is here to support the Melina Foundation.' Ares smiled.

Gia stiffened.

Bethan had no idea what the Melina Foundation was, but it clearly bothered Gia. She should have made it clear that she was here only to formalise their divorce. Instead she'd let embarrassment silence her.

Gia's frown deepened. 'I don't understand—'

'Our relationship has always been different,' he interrupted Gia bluntly. 'Always very special.'

Bethan quelled her shiver. He didn't mean that in the desperately romantic way it sounded. His thumb stroked back and forth across her shoulder. The tiny insistent sweeps would send her into ecstatic orbit if they were alone. As it was goosebumps lifted on her skin—those gentlest of touches softened her all over again, even though she was wildly angry with him. Chemistry had so much to answer for.

'I'm sure you'll forgive our early departure now. You understand it's a while since we spent quality time together. We only had a quickly snatched moment to reunite before remembering to call in here and...' He shrugged negligently and shot Bethan a scorching look that she knew not to misinterpret. 'Time alone is our priority tonight.'

CHAPTER FOUR

How *dared* she?

Ares refused to swear, which meant he couldn't actually breathe. If he opened his mouth there'd be an outpouring of vitriol and that was not happening in front of his damned 'family' let alone all these business connections. He hugged Bethan close, swiftly leading her back to the elevator. He kept holding his breath as they finally descended to the basement. His waiting driver glanced up as they walked towards the car, read his expression and immediately fired the engine and activated the privacy screen.

'What was *that*?' Bethan shot the second they got in the car.

'*You're* angry with *me*?' Ares retorted as he messaged his driver his instruction.

'You all but admitted what we'd been...'

Ares's brain slid off course, distracted by the discovery she still blushed when discussing sex. He dragged in a deep breath and forced focus.

'*You're* the one who said that we're together,' he goaded, furious she'd let those people believe something so outrageous. 'I was being supportive and not contradicting you in public, like the good husband I am.'

Her eyes flashed. 'Did you stop the elevator on that floor deliberately?'

'What?' Why would he ever? And how could she even think something so crazy? Stunned, he just snapped. 'Of course not.'

He swore, long and loud in Greek, and it barely released any of his frustration. He'd been too distracted to notice *anything*—frustrated as hell because he'd seen a harrowing hurt in her eyes that he still didn't understand. Because he *had* pleased her—she'd been wet and hot and she'd chanted his name as her orgasm hit. Pleasing her was so bloody rewarding, but that best of moments had turned to acrid, bitter ash in seconds because he'd been unable to see it through. He would *never* run the risk of impregnating her. He was never having children. A failure of a son to his mother, he would be a failure of a father too—as his had been to him. For a few days just over two years ago he'd thought he could fake it—but then Bethan had questioned and he'd been unable to answer.

But in all this current mess, he'd completely forgotten there were drinks at the office for clients tonight. Stepping into that room had been an automatic response because he was Ares Vasiliadis—in control and unaffected, high-performing heir and CEO. He'd been whipped into shape by that damned dysfunctional family in less than five years and he would never do less than excel in front of them. He would always remain in control around them.

He'd seen Gia and Dion home in on Bethan like circling sharks. He'd been about to intervene but he'd briefly stilled because Bethan's chin had lifted. She'd smiled—so politely, so confidently. Her cheeks had still been flushed from passion and her eyes had gleamed proud—magnificently. He'd been awed by her quiet dignity until he'd come to his senses and stepped in. Too late, damage done. They'd needled her.

He'd not been bothered by *them*. He was immune to their reluctant tolerance and wouldn't give them power. Not showing a hit—a hurt—had never been a problem until Bethan. But somehow a poker face was impossible around her. *Her* belief he'd set that elevator to open on that floor got beneath his armour and he was too outraged to hide it.

'You really don't trust me,' he said bitterly. 'Why would I want any of them to see me with you again?'

'Maybe it wasn't about them.' Her expression pinched. 'Maybe it was about humiliating me because you're still angry I walked out on you.'

He was *wildly* angry with her, but not for that reason. His problem was that he still wanted her to a shockingly uncontrollable degree.

'So you told them we're back together?' he growled, stuck in a maelstrom of conflicting emotion.

He couldn't believe the chaos she'd caused in a few minutes. She'd turned an already difficult situation into a public spectacle at the worst possible time.

'I didn't tell them, they *saw* us,' she argued. 'What was I supposed to do?'

'Be honest,' he snapped.

'I *was*,' she shot back. 'And you were the one getting handsy in the elevator.'

He glared at her, which was unhelpful given she was infuriatingly beautiful. And yes, she probably hadn't told anyone she was back with him. Gia would have manipulated the moment, just as she tried to manipulate everything. And he hadn't been getting 'handsy' with Bethan, he'd wanted to know if she was okay. Why did he damned well even care?

Because now *he* wasn't okay. He wasn't able to stop thinking about how she'd gone up in flames in his office. How swiftly he'd lost control. How soft and hot she'd felt. How badly he'd wanted to pin her beneath him and take her but he couldn't because no way in hell was he ever having children. They didn't need the baggage he would rain down on them. His whole family were fucked and he refused to screw up more innocent kids.

All he wanted was to expunge this insane desire. He was irate it still burned like this. But he needed to focus on fixing the mess she'd just made. He'd told them Bethan was here for the Melina Foundation, so she would have to attend because he was allowing nothing and no one to ruin that night.

Bethan would have to stay for all of this *week*. His bitter frustration simply fuelled the satisfaction that thought brought. They had unfinished business. Maybe he would drive her mad with want for him. Maybe he would make her forget any other man she'd had in her bed. Maybe he would destroy her for any more to come…because he *absolutely* could. It was what she'd already done to him.

His pulse settled into a happy rhythm as he formulated a plan. He would demand this week. It would well be long enough for him to have his cake and eat it too.

'Where are we going?' Bethan sharply interrupted his thoughts. 'I need to go to a hotel.'

He clenched his jaw. 'We're going to my place.'

'No.' She stiffened. 'I'm not going back to that compound. Ever.'

Her vehemence surprised him—yet resonated. The Vasiliadis compound was a palatial residence in the wealthiest suburb in Athens with additional residences either side. It had everything, from home cinema, to tennis court, *two* pools, and more. Of course Bethan would disapprove of the over-the-top consumerist consumption. While it was filled with riches it was empty of anything warm. It was also full of bad memories— she'd spent three days there but he'd endured it from the age of thirteen. Move-in day had been the loneliest moment of his life. Cut off from contacting his mother, he'd been too hurt, too proud, too stubborn to break that rule. Gia hadn't wanted anything to do with him of course. He'd been isolated, ignored other than to be instructed. He'd been brought there to learn everything necessary to be the worthy heir. Despite the fact a bunch of distant cousins lived onsite, he'd been isolated and relentlessly schooled. And it was where *they'd* argued. Where she'd walked out and boarded the first flight back to Britain. Ares hated the place and sure as hell didn't live there any more.

'Bethan.' He inhaled sharply, shutting down those memories. 'Your "loving wife" act just now changed everything. We need to keep our issues discreet. I am trying to protect—'

'I don't need your protection.'

'This time it's not about *you*,' he shouted.

And he did *not* want to hear her declare yet again that she needed or wanted nothing from him.

'We'll talk when we get to my place and it is not the compound,' he growled.

They needed privacy and space and he was barely able to contain the energy firing around him. Because he would win this.

Gia, Dion and the other board members bowed to his opinions, given how well the company was doing under his command, but his 'little charitable endeavour', as they'd called it, was deeply personal. They loathed the fact, but the Vasiliadis family would be forced to acknowledge his mother's existence. Ares would remind them all not just of his illegitimacy but of his authority. There was *nothing* they could do to stop him doing this now. Because for years he'd not been allowed to mention her, he'd not even *seen* her—not gaining the strength until it was too late. But now her name would literally be in lights and in future he wouldn't allow anyone to be treated the way his mother had been treated by them. Their 'dirty little secret' would be dragged from the shadows.

He needed to do this—needed something to ease his guilt because he'd left her—left it all—too late. So he would have nothing taint the moment he finally, publicly honoured Melina and if that meant having to have Bethan by his side for the evening, so be it. The thought actually made him feel slightly better about the whole thing. Probably because she was his side order of seduction and yeah, he was still a selfish jerk.

Fifteen minutes later he watched her pace about his lounge, her face a picture of displeasure.

'Why don't you live at the compound?' she asked irritably.

'This is closer to work,' he muttered shortly.

True enough but not the real reason. He'd bought a penthouse in the city after Bethan had walked out and, honestly, he didn't like her here. He'd never associated this place with her presence but now it was marked forever. He made a mental note to get his agent to put it on the market next week.

'I'm not staying with you, Ares. You can't keep me here. I'm calling a—'

He barred her headlong exit with his body. He was so very tired of her defiance already. 'Just don't, Bethan.'

She glared up into his eyes, clearly spoiling for a fight. He was too. Their unstoppable chemistry still burned out of control. And if it wasn't lust, it was anger. But he would resist.

He made himself step back, holding up his hands. 'You'll have your own room. Surely you can compromise?'

'No.'

Ah, there was the rejection again and he was so tempted to prove just how *willing* he could get her in about three minutes flat. 'You're the one who started this, Bethan. I just wanted you here to get the paperwork done with the notary.'

'Right, that's why you launched on me the second you got me alone.'

'Oh, so in your world, *I'm* the one who started it? I get to be the bad guy who took advantage.'

'Again. Yes.'

'Because you somehow lost the ability to say no? You're so good at lying to yourself. I didn't do anything you didn't beg for. In fact I'm pretty sure you were begging me to do even more.'

She pressed her lips together tightly and quite obviously counted to three.

'Then what is it *you* want?' she finally muttered. 'Why have you dragged me here?'

Well, she'd hardly been kicking and screaming. He couldn't help smirking—actually she *had* been screaming his name less than an hour ago. 'Your ill-judged decision not to make our lack of relationship clear to my business associates has ramifications that you're going to have to endure for a little while longer.'

'Your business associates? Wasn't that your stepmother?'

'Gia is no kind of mother to me and never has been.'

His snap instantly silenced her. In fact Bethan looked stunned.

Ares felt a qualm inside. Yeah, that was about the most he'd told her about his relationship with Gia. But honestly he'd thought his distance from Gia and the rest would be obvious, given he didn't spend time with them. Plus he'd simply assumed Bethan's loyalty in any interactions. Perhaps that hadn't been fair. There was no doubt her family would have been wildly different. But the Vasiliadises didn't discuss family—indeed anything personal—with anyone. They were too proud, too powerful. The sheer dysfunction was kept behind closed doors. He'd taken their lessons deep. Say nothing. But he would *do* it all now—show not tell. Only that was what he'd thought he'd done back then…

Bethan circled like a sparring opponent sizing him up before striking her blow. 'What are the ramifications?'

He took a moment to focus. 'Next Friday there's an important gala at the headquarters. Nothing and no one will overshadow the success of that night so you'll remain here this week and attend—gracious and smiling.'

Her jaw dropped. 'Why on earth would you want me there?'

'Because I said you would be and now it's expected. If you don't show up, then it will be a distraction.'

'Won't it be more of a distraction if I *am* there?'

His fury mounted. He'd never intended to tell her how personally important the foundation was to him. Acknowledging that felt like weakness. She might use it against him and he didn't trust her. Or anyone. 'You'll quietly accompany me and afterwards you'll discreetly disappear again.'

'Did I discreetly disappear last time? What did you tell people?'

He'd said nothing, as it happened. As always. He'd iced up when people asked and people had stopped asking very quickly.

She cleared her throat when he didn't answer. 'I didn't think you cared about what others think.'

'I don't, other than in connection to the business.'

'It really is all about the money for you,' she said caustically.

'It is the *one* constant in my life,' he agreed glibly.

And that was true—money had been at the core of everything. The lack of it when he'd been young and still living with his mother. The endless amount when his father had died and his grandfather had been hell-bent on securing a direct blood heir. Money had brought him freedom and was one thing he'd truly been successful at in spite of them all. Including her.

'What about Sophia?' she muttered, twisting her bangle.

'What about her?' He tilted his head, confused by the change in topic.

Bethan cleared her throat. 'I saw her engagement ring.'

Her what? Ares stilled. 'And you thought *I* gave it to her?' Amazed, he watched Bethan avoid his eyes and couldn't contain a small chuckle. 'Are you jealous of Sophia?'

Oh, this was good. That she was territorial over him, sexually at least, felt fantastic and was a little payback for how jealous he'd felt of that man she'd dined with last night. He savoured it a second longer before relenting. 'Sophia is engaged to someone else.'

The tips of Bethan's ears reddened. 'So you expect me to stay in Greece for an additional week just to show up at one of your work functions.'

'I think it's the least you can do.' He wanted to win *something* here.

She would be his wife for one more week—superficially a convenient arrangement to suppress scandal, but still his wife. They would see this out in *every* way. What had happened during their separation wasn't his business, but these next few days, she would be his. Only his.

'You will do it, Bethan.' He leaned forward, reckless

determination pouring through him. 'Because if you don't pose as my happily reconciled wife for the next week and come to the gala, then I'll argue that we've been together this whole time. That will reset the clock for our divorce. Two more years tied to me, you ready for that?'

'You're dreaming,' Bethan said scathingly, unable to believe her ears. 'No one will ever believe we've *not* been separated. I've been living in London.'

'And I've made frequent trips to London over the last two years.' He smiled at her evilly. 'Who's to say you weren't in my bed each and every one of the nights I was there?'

Her heart thudded. 'I am,' she whispered. 'I will say that.'

And she was devastated to learn that he'd been to London that often and known where she was yet never been tempted to see her. She actually felt cut off at the knees and had to sit down to hide the hit of weakness.

'So it will be your word against mine.' He cocked his head and took the seat opposite. 'I have dates. Hotel receipts—'

'Proof of female company there?'

'You know the answer to that already. I have the best lawyers—can you even afford a lawyer?' He jeered. 'I can create doubt. They'll believe me.'

'Because you'll shamelessly lie?'

'In this particular instance, I'll do whatever it takes.'

'To get what you want.' She shook her head.

He *always* got what he wanted. And he had no qualms about lying. Apparently it was effortless for him.

'You *really* want me at this party?' she asked after another pregnant moment.

'Yes.'

Clearly she was missing something. Ares needed no one's support or approval—ever.

'Why is this one so important?' she asked.

'If you stay, then, the second the gala is over, I won't contest the divorce. In fact I'll ensure the process is expedited. We will go to the notary first thing, the morning after.'

It was so incredibly important, he'd just completely avoided answering. And she was utterly intrigued.

She considered her options. 'I want it in writing that this one week won't delay our divorce at all.'

His tension eased. 'Sure. We can even itemise what can and cannot happen between us in this next week.'

'*Nothing* else is going to happen between us.' But she couldn't suppress an inner flare of anticipation. At the very least she would spar with him for the next week. Hell, she wanted to win one over him.

'Nothing you don't want to happen, no.' He smiled as if he knew. 'But you're lying to yourself. We both know something will happen again. It's always been like this with us and maybe it will remain like this unless we do something to get rid of it. Maybe we should be realistic about what happens when we get near to each other.'

'Maybe we should admit that's more reason to get apart quickly and *stay* apart.'

'You'll still ache for me,' he said.

Bethan looked at him. Quiet. Compelling. *Correct.* Maybe she would always ache for him but that moment in his office tonight had scalded her in a way she wasn't sure she could survive a second time. It wasn't about denying him. It was about saving herself.

His gaze narrowed. 'Just to make it clear, you won't be going on any other dates this week.'

'Just to make it clear, the same applies to you.'

'As I've already said, I've been utterly faithful to you this entire time.'

She sent him a sceptical look. 'I thought you were just being dramatic.'

He stretched out, apparently calm, but she knew he was more tense than he was trying to appear. Her rebellion built the longer he didn't respond. He'd said some, but not enough and still she ached. Why *him*? Why only ever him?

'What is it about this particular event that's so special?' She was determined to find out and so twisted the one blade she had. 'Or is it just a tragic excuse to force me to spend more time with you this week because you want your last bit of me?'

His eyes bored into hers—a flicker of fire.

'Because that isn't going to happen,' she added. Far too late.

His smile appeared—infuriatingly knowing. 'Whatever you say.'

Blood rushed, burning the back of her neck. 'Isn't it better for me to know so I can ensure to behave accordingly?'

'I'm sure you'll behave perfectly adequately.'

'Wow. Faint praise.' She swallowed. 'You said I didn't trust you and maybe there's some truth to that but, given you won't tell me, you don't trust me either. You never have—you didn't trust me before I walked out.'

The heat in his eyes flared to anger. But it was true. He'd not told her anything about his family other than that both his parents were dead. He'd not explained the nuances about his stepmother, the reasons why things were so obviously frosty.

'So how do you want this week to work?' She pushed on before he could snap—before her own anger unravelled. 'Are we going to go to fancy dinners? Spending time with your friends? Because you didn't want me to do any of that with you the last time we were married. You wanted me to stay locked up on the island villa, living a quiet life that you came and went from, remember?' She bit her lip sharply. 'And how do I explain our choice to spend so much time apart? Do I tell them all I went to London to start my career as a *cleaner*? Won't *that* little detail overshadow your important event?'

But he didn't bite. 'Cleaning is honest work, Bethan.' He tensed, focused on that last. 'Nothing to be ashamed about.'

'It's beneath your family's status.' There was an army of cleaners at that compound. The wealthy operated in a different realm.

'My mother was a cleaner,' he said softly.

Bethan gaped. She'd not known that but of course she'd known little of his childhood. They'd bonded over being orphans but both skipped over detail—too busy connecting on a physical level dancing in the waves, in the sheets. Lost in the intoxication of each other. And she at least hadn't wanted to bring that mood down. She'd thought it would all come out eventually, given they were 'soulmates'...

'The foundation is in honour of her,' Ares added quietly. 'She died several years ago. I think I told you that.'

She had a sharp flash of comprehension. 'She's Melina.'

'Yes.'

She'd not even known his mother's name. They'd made so many mistakes.

'Some in the family don't want the Vasiliadis name to be associated with it,' he added stiffly. 'My half-brother, Alex, and I were only a couple of months apart in age. Gia doesn't like to be reminded of my father's infidelity but I don't like what happened to my mother to be forgotten.'

His *half-brother*? Bethan was completely confused. She'd assumed Gia had been his father's second wife—that she'd married Ares's father after his mother's death. But she'd not asked and Ares hadn't said. This was fundamental.

'What happened to her?' she asked. And *where* was this Alex?

That calm, emotional mask descended over Ares's hard sculpted features. He wasn't going to answer. She glanced down at her empty hands.

'She was taken advantage of by an older, married man.' His words were soft. 'When she got pregnant he abandoned her. Her fledgling career was destroyed and she was burdened with her mistake for the rest of her life.' He rolled his shoulders and stood. 'I don't know about you but it's past time for food.'

Almost numb, Bethan followed him to the kitchen, where he began pulling containers from the fridge and covered dishes from the oven, setting them on the dining table in the corner. He added a couple of plates, grabbed a couple of glasses. But she turned over what he'd said and the more she thought about it, the more concerned she grew.

'Why didn't you tell me any of this before?' she asked. But what she'd said was true. He hadn't trusted her.

'I don't discuss it with anyone.' He fished in a cutlery drawer.

'I was your *wife*.' She couldn't hold back her hurt whisper.

He paused, glancing across at her. 'And was there nothing you kept from me back then, Bethan?'

She stared back helplessly. Because there had been. She'd been reluctant to share her past with him then. Her grief had been too raw. She'd not wanted to drag down those heady days—they'd been a delirious, passionate *escape*. She'd figured it would all come out eventually, only she'd dropped down to earth with a bump. But now, now she realised this was more complicated than her loss. She thought about the way he'd changed around his family. And that time he'd changed around *her*. The cold mask that had dropped so quickly and easily.

He opened the containers and began serving food onto his plate. 'You can go on a hunger strike if you want, but I'm too famished to fight more right now.'

Bethan took the seat across from his. The dishes he'd pulled were her favourites. But it wasn't that he'd remembered and done that deliberately, it was that she had pretty basic tastes. The trouble was there were memories attached to these tastes. As she nibbled she remembered the warmth of those long days and even longer nights. But the food also helped settle her wired system and helped her *think*. She'd learned more about him in the last few minutes than she'd learned in the entire time they'd been together years ago. She needed to know more. Understand more. Because it might help her resolve this. But not only did she feel more curious, she also felt more inclined to support him.

They both finished their plates silently. He seemingly as lost in thought as she. Eventually she stood, helped clear the dishes, then turned to him.

'Will you show me which room I can use?' she asked.

He wiped his hands then tossed the cloth onto the counter. 'So you'll stay.'

'For the gala, yes.' She couldn't resist that soaring curiosity.

Besides, she was doing it for his mother—a woman hurt and alone and who—for more reasons than Bethan was sure he'd admitted—he wanted to honour. She respected him for that.

And if Gia had been no kind of parent to him, Ares had been alone too. Unless his half-brother had been there? What had happened in that horribly cold compound that had made him so closed off? Maybe if she understood him more, she might be at peace with why they'd not worked out. Maybe this week would help her actually get over him.

She followed him through the apartment. It was large and she could keep her distance easily enough. Presumably he'd be at work during the day, so it mightn't be that bad at all. He paused by a door and gestured. She glanced in and saw her bag was already there. He'd expected her acquiescence and his assistant had quietly arranged everything.

'I'll go to any other events you deem necessary this week,' she offered huskily.

For a moment too long, he hesitated. She watched heat kindle in his eyes and stepped back even as answering cinders ignited inside her. Yes, the lust was still there but he wanted to get *rid* of it because he didn't really want *her*.

'Then we divorce,' she added, reminding herself as much as him. 'Because nothing is going to happen between us again.'

CHAPTER FIVE

'Bethan?'

'Mmm?' Bethan stretched languorously and snuggled deeper. She knew this was a dream, but now she was finally on the edge of sleep, she didn't have the strength to resist responding to the sultry whisper.

'Bethan.'

This time impatience iced the heat she'd heard. She blinked blearily and clocked Ares standing beside her bed, coffee mug in hand. Full consciousness slammed. Not a dream. A disaster. She swiftly sat up, pulling the coverings with her. 'What's going on?'

He set the mug on the table beside her and stepped back, his arms folded across his chest. 'I thought about what you said and you were right.'

Only Ares could concede a point with such an air of imperious condescension.

'Of course I was.' Still dazed, Bethan reached for the coffee and racked her brains before soon capitulating. 'Which bit was I right about?'

His grin flashed too briefly. 'I don't want you to go to dinner parties in Athens with me this week. Because I don't want to go to them. I never do. It's long been a source of friction with my family and is partly why they wanted me to take a wife who would conform to their social requirements.'

Bethan studied the steam rising from the coffee as she processed that. 'You never went to those dinner parties?'

'I went to some years ago but haven't in years. The family wanted me to do a lot of things I had little interest in.' He paused for effect. 'Like Sophia Dimou.'

Heat surging in her cheeks, she glanced up in time to see his smug smile. She'd been so jealous of that beautiful young woman for so long. And she'd assumed he didn't want to take her to fancy dinner parties because she wouldn't fit into their rarefied society—the horrors of high-school tormentors had long ago destroyed her self-esteem in that area.

'Anyway, the simplest thing is to spend this week at the villa on Avra,' he said.

'What?' She jerked, splashing coffee on the back of her hand as all thoughts of Sophia fled.

He frowned and snatched up the towel she'd left draped on the back of a chair. 'It's private, the weather is better and the time will pass quickly.'

Um. No. She did *not* want to return to that villa. At least, not with him. She'd tried to forget its beauty but couldn't. Hell, she'd even made artwork based on her memories of it.

'You'll be working here in Athens,' she muttered as he firmly took her hand and wiped away the scalding coffee.

It had only been a splash, there would be no mark, but she didn't seem to have the strength to tell him, or take the towel and do it herself.

'Oh no. I'll be there with you.' He inspected her skin—too close, too concerned, too *much*. 'We'll leak some pictures to prove our ecstasy.'

She curled her fingers and slipped her hand free of his. 'But you have a gala to organise.'

'It's already organised—not by me—and I can do my work remotely. I've done that before, if you recall.' His smile was sharp. 'It's perfect, no?'

'Not for me, no.' She groped for a reason to reject his plan. 'I have work to do.'

'And you can do it on the island.'

'Unlike you, I need more than a computer. I need supplies. I have a half-finished piece—'

'You mean a prop? I'll send the jet to get whatever you need from London. Let's just get to the island and arrange it from there.' His gaze hardened. 'We'll go by helicopter. It'll be faster.'

She gaped. He knew about her work. 'I don't have—'

'Whatever it is you need, Bethan, it can be bought.'

And that was where they differed. He thought money could buy anything. But it couldn't. Not what she *really* needed.

Two hours later she gazed at the stunning view of sapphire waters dotted with emerald and topaz islands. It was heart-rendingly beautiful—a true paradise. And then Avra came into view. They passed over the small village clinging to the top of the steep hill. That first day they'd sat in the shade at that quiet taverna for several hours. He'd help her book a room at the adjacent hotel so she could stay the night. One night had turned into a week. She'd been amazed that the place wasn't overrun with tourists. He'd told her the rich stayed at resorts, not the small villages, or visited briefly on their luxury boats. That not many 'ordinary tourists' made the difficult journey to get there, given there were party islands and equally picturesque places that were far easier to get to. Back then she'd been the kind of naïve person who took people at face value and believed what they told her.

It was almost a week before she'd learned the truth—that the *truly* wealthy—like him—had their *own* private resorts. Because he moved her into his enormous property. The stunning villa overlooked the coast, enhanced by terraced gardens and patios, an infinity pool and spa and a gorgeous curling path that led to the sheltered postcard-perfect beach. It was at that beach where the local mayor had married them in a fifteen-minute ceremony, having expedited the paperwork for his favourite resident.

When the helicopter touched down, Bethan stepped out and quickly moved clear. The gardens were still gorgeous—the plants those hardy herby sorts that thrived in heat and salt-kissed sea air. The villa was as stunning as she remembered too—white walls, warm stone, the neutral furnishings creating a cool yet cosy feel. The place was restful yet also designed for play. She knew there were water toys galore in the boat shed just up from the beach. Paddle boards, snorkels, jet ski, a solo-handing sailboat and more…she and Ares had used them all when they'd been here last. Their love for the water was probably their one true commonality. Aside from a hyper sex drive. Although *that* she'd only discovered with him. Because of him.

She drew a breath. There would be no repeat of those mistakes—that 'magic' couldn't be recaptured. They'd taken a holiday fling too far and at the same time held too much back.

'You take this room.' He slung her small bag inside the bedroom they'd shared. 'I prefer one on the other side.'

He walked out before she could argue. Her cheeks scalded as she gazed at the enormous bed. They'd had their wedding night here. She'd barely slept.

Needing to splash water on her face, she walked through the dressing room to get to the bathroom. She didn't get there. She stopped, stunned at the sight of the clothing hanging on the rail. *Her* dresses were still here—including the silk she'd worn while barefoot on the beach for their wedding. Heart ricocheting, she opened the top drawer. Her bikini was neatly folded on the top—the black and white animal-print one she'd thought herself so bold in buying for that once-in-a-lifetime holiday. *All* of the clothes she'd brought with her and the ones he'd bought her in that time were still here—not just the wedding dress but the lace shawl she'd admired in the local village. He'd arranged for her to spend time with the woman who'd made it for an afternoon and it had been amazing.

Breathlessly she ran a flannel beneath cold water, battling the sinking feeling she was right back where she'd started—trapped inside a total infatuation. Just being near him destroyed her brain but she couldn't let herself fall for him again. She knew now how good at masking he was—that he was cold inside. And yes, calculating. His desire for her to be at the gala *was* calculating and while maybe he had valid reasons, her understanding them wouldn't make him any less so. The fact was his work mattered more to him than anything. More to him than family. He'd not loved her the way she'd needed to be loved. Honestly, she didn't know if he could love anyone in that way. That couldn't be her problem again. She couldn't change him but she could change herself—she *had*. She'd wised up and now she just had to stay strong and understand that all they'd had was nothing deeper than intense physical chemistry. But she couldn't let herself have him again because then she would want the more he couldn't give. She'd lost enough already and now she had a good life that she wasn't going to jeopardise just for lust.

She stuffed her notebook, pens and knitting into her tote. She would continue working on the blanket for Phoebe's baby, maybe start a jersey and sketch props ideas. She'd been bluffing about having urgent work. If she kept busy the time would go quickly and—heartbreakingly—she'd always found this place creatively inspiring. Assuming he'd be working in the study, she went out to the infinity pool. And skidded to a stop. In swim shorts and nothing else, Ares was clearly about to dive in. But he caught sight of her and didn't.

His gaze nailed her to the spot. As did his beauty. It was so unfair that he was this lethally good-looking.

'All okay?' he asked.

She nodded, battling the intensity of his scrutiny, unable to bring herself to ask why he'd kept her entire wardrobe here. It wouldn't have been for any *special* reason. He'd probably just been too busy to be bothered.

'Um.' She needed an escape. 'I'm going to work in the lounge, it's too hot out here.'

He was too hot.

'There's a studio you can use if you would prefer,' he said. 'Your own space. This way.'

Unable to resist, she followed him, taking in the endless blue shades of pool, ocean, sky—thankful because it gave her something to stare at instead of Ares's tanned, muscular frame and the lithe grace with which he moved. In truth that brilliant blue vista had been seared on her memory and was a constant inspiration. She'd made several sculptures using those colours as an ode to this place—trying to exorcise the heart-aching beauty of it from her soul. One of those pieces had been the one she'd sold.

'Here.' Ares opened a door.

She'd thought this building on the further side of the pool was a guest house or staff quarters. Indeed perhaps this large, cool room had once been a lounge but now it was undeniably an artist's studio. She stared at the floor-to-ceiling shelves running along the back wall—many filled with a shocking array of unopened packages. The labels identified them—not just paints and pencils, but tools. A sewing machine on the table. Assorted scissors in a block. There was even a pottery wheel. Bethan worked with multi-media and this enormous workroom was...almost complete. There was a large worktable with a lamp. Another desk. A low, obviously comfortable armchair. He'd made this paradise of an island home even more perfect—this was the sort of place she could spend hours in, like the shed at her grandmother's cottage.

'You liked crafts, I built you a studio. I'm not sure if there's everything you need for your project but, as I said, we can pick up anything else you need from London.'

She hardly heard him, too busy being astounded. She moved deeper into the absolute arcadia, angling her head to read a smaller label. 'When did you have this done?'

'It was to be your wedding present but you never came back here to see it.'

Bethan turned, her lungs tight. He'd leaned back, gripping the edge of the counter, a vision of bronzed skin and tense, rippling muscles. Why hadn't he gotten rid of it?

'I haven't been back here much either,' he added in a low mutter.

'Busy with work.'

'Yes.'

How could he be so thoughtful and yet so remote?

'You confuse me,' she murmured.

'Don't read anything into it,' he said gruffly. 'I wanted you to be happy here.'

Happy. *Here*. Not in Athens. Not actually *with* him through the week. That old bitter, bereft ache rose. And this room was separate from the main house—again, *away* from him. He mightn't like those dinner parties, but he'd still wanted distance from her. While part of him was so generous, this place would have suited him too. Suited him best.

'This will be a perfect refuge this week,' she said stiffly, hoping he'd take the hint and leave. 'Thank you.'

Refuge. Ares gripped the edge of the workbench more tightly to lock himself in place. He wasn't about to leave even when that was obviously what she wanted. Nor was he about to grab her and make her swallow her falsely polite-as-hell *thanks*. Since when was Bethan either sarcastic or cynical?

Since walking out on him.

She bent her head so all he could see was her glossy hair and all he could do was keep staring. He should be *pleased* by this situation. He'd exerted the smallest amount of control, exacting the slightest hint of revenge by requiring her to remain here in the place she'd rejected, meaning she wouldn't have her own way for just a little bit longer, and it meant that their goodbye would be on his terms at a time he wasn't just prepared for but was relishing. He should be delighted that soon she would leave his life for ever, no? More than that, he should be triumphant because he knew she still *wanted* him.

There should be no risk here, only reward. Yet he felt coarsely uncomfortable.

Why had he left this studio stocked and ready for all this time? When he'd known she wouldn't be back. When he'd known she wasn't into material things or great displays of expense. Why had he shown her now? Had he thought he'd get pleasure from showing her what she'd walked out on? Because he didn't. Instead he felt… weak. Because he'd just left it. Unable to look at it. Unable to move her clothes as well, he now remembered. What kind of pathetic fool was he?

But she'd been a fool too. She'd been jealous of *Sophia*. That revelation had circled round his head all night and still was a small consolation now. Sophia Dimou was his stepmother Gia's niece—almost a cousin though not by blood. The family had suggested that Sophia would be the perfect wife to ensure Ares's place in society was assured and polished. It was a play for control to keep their influence over him. Make him more palatable—less of a *fraud*.

He'd known her for years—even kissed her a long time ago. It had instantly told them all they'd needed to know. Hard *no*. Never in a million years would he agree, no matter how much pressure—even publicly—they brought to bear. However, Sophia hadn't the strength to stand up to her family for a long time. Ares was genuinely pleased she'd finally found happiness with someone else. But apparently her existence had caused Bethan angst. How had Bethan even known about her? The same way Bethan had thought he'd want to waste time at tedious dinner parties with boring people. Someone had told her and he even knew who.

'Why did you pay so much attention to what Gia said?' he asked. 'Why would you trust the word of a woman you barely knew?'

Bethan turned from her exploration of some of the packages. 'She's your family,' she said simply. Sadly. 'I thought she was being honest with me so I could support you.'

A sinking sensation sucked him. *He* wouldn't trust but Bethan had a wildly different background. Regret curled. 'She mentioned Sophia to you.'

She still avoided his gaze. 'She said your engagement was well publicised and wanted to warn me in case someone said something. So I looked it up. Google translated all those stories in the society pages. Some of them were years old.'

But even those articles didn't tell the whole truth and the whispers of his background had been wiped from the web. Gia's 'warning' had in fact been an attack. He should have prepared her. Instead he'd kept so much from her. It had been habit, no? And self-protection. Keeping his past private had been a requirement and he'd never wanted to answer questions about his mother anyway. Just thinking about her had hurt too much because of the guilt he carried for his part in her demise. He'd never wanted to admit his failure to anyone, let alone to Bethan. He'd shut down that entire part of himself. But not any more—hence the foundation. He needed to make reparations there. Perhaps here too.

'I became Ares Vasiliadis when I was thirteen years old,' he suddenly admitted. 'Before that, I was Ares Pappas, the unwanted and illegitimate son of Loukas Vasiliadis.'

Her eyes widened. 'What?'

Pushing past old habits was uncomfortable but this little she deserved to know—why Gia had been so unkind. That it wasn't *her*. 'Pavlos Vasiliadis—Loukas's father—cared about nothing more than his bloodline and when my father and half-brother died unexpectedly, I was swept in as Pavlos's replacement grandson and heir.'

'You...' She stared at him. 'You're not joking, are you?'

'Pavlos was completely controlling. Everyone followed his edicts. He had power, money and far-reaching influence. They changed my name, changed my school, changed my life.'

'They wanted you to do everything they asked,' she said slowly. 'But you refused regarding Sophia.'

Regarding so many things, actually. Sophia was the least of it. But Bethan was locked on her and it was welcome. Her fixation on her saved him from dwelling on the deeper wounds of the half-brother he'd never gotten to know, the bitter wrath of his stepmother, the pain of his mother's abandonment.

'You resisted that engagement for so long but then married me super quick. Was it to shake off the pressure they were putting on you?'

He hesitated. If he'd realised anything in the past twenty-four hours, it was that they'd not communicated honestly enough. It didn't feel right to hold back on her now. 'There are multiple benefits to any deal.'

'So our marriage was a "deal".' Emotion bloomed in her eyes.

'One that could have worked well,' he said tightly. 'You were alone—'

'So you *pitied* me. You thought you were doing me a favour.'

Why was she getting angry?

'And I was. I could give you things you never would have had otherwise,' he growled, frustrated by her hurt accusation. 'You expect me to separate out issues that are too tangled. Truth is I wanted you. I didn't want her. I thought it would work. I thought it would be easy.'

Because it *had* been easy. He'd thought *keeping* her happy would keep being easy. Full truth—he hadn't really thought at all. He'd been impulsive. He'd wanted to keep her in his bed. Wanted to keep sailing with her— those days on the beach all the fun he'd not had in years. Not since he'd been a carefree kid relishing the rare days when his hardworking solo mother had had the time to shed her stress and taken him to the beach and taught him how to swim and sail.

'Why weren't you honest with me about all this back then?' she asked. 'Why keep it so secret?'

'It wasn't a conscious thing.' He kept everything quiet. 'It happened fast.' He'd just gone for it. 'I wanted it to be on my terms. My choice.'

'So I was just in the right place at the right time.'

'You really think that?' He gaped.

'I think you trifled with my emotions.'

'I *married* you.'

'*Not* because you loved me.'

He stilled—on the precipice of the same cliff he'd fallen off years ago. When she'd asked this and he'd not answered. He'd not lied to her. But that was not what she'd wanted.

He didn't believe the kind of love she dreamed of. Lust, yes. Safe companionship maybe. But love? That was a lie.

'You thought I'd be a compliant wife.' Her face was pale. 'You thought you could control me the way they tried to control you.'

Fury flared. 'I *never* wanted to control you.'

'You wanted to tuck me away.' Her anger matched his. 'Why? So you could have affairs without me knowing?'

He'd wanted her to be *happy*. And she'd been happy here.

'Why would you even think that?' he asked. There had never been anyone else.

She was too furious to listen. 'You thought I was so insipid—so infatuated—that I'd do anything you wanted me to.'

He frowned. 'I never thought of you that way.'

'No?' She moved closer. 'Then how *did* you think of me?'

That she was sweet. Okay, yes, easy to please. That maybe he could care for her enough. That he would be enough as he was—stunted. That maybe he would not fail her as he'd failed in the past. But she'd walked out at the first hurdle. And there was no point raking over the past. It changed nothing. He was who he was. So he shut her down. 'It doesn't matter now, does it?'

'Doesn't it?' Her anger exploded. '*I'm* asking. Or does what *I* want not matter?'

He thought he'd done so much for her, but most had been based on assumptions that only now he realised were wrong.

'You didn't want me to *live* with you in Athens,' she said, hurt sharpening her tone. 'You wanted to be a part-time husband. You didn't want anything to upset your perfectly curated world. You didn't go to the dinners and you thought you could stick it to them even more by marrying someone utterly inappropriate.'

'You were *never* not good enough.' How could she think that?

'No?' She laughed bitterly. 'Which is why in the one week in which you've decided to endure me as your wife again, you've brought me back here where no one can see us. Why can't you just admit you're ashamed of me?'

'That's *not* what this is.' He wanted to shake some sense into her. Hold her firm and still so she had to listen. But his hands slid around her waist, pulled her close and threw the rest of him back into chaos.

'No?' Bitterness sharpened in her eyes. 'Then it's just this—you still just want to screw me.'

Lust overwhelmed him. 'I'm not alone in wanting that.' He pressed her closer, feeling her soften even as she glared up at him with those beautiful, angry eyes.

His gaze dropped to her pout. He was a second from spinning and pinning her to that table with his hips, desperately aching for the abandonment, the utter oblivion that lust brought them. He craved that bliss in which nothing else mattered.

'Well, it's not happening,' she breathed. '*That* is not part of this deal.'

CHAPTER SIX

BETHAN SPENT A sleepless night in the bed that was far too big without him, ruminating on his revelations. Where had he been before being taken into that family? What had happened to his father and half-brother? Why was it all so obviously wretched? She'd not told him some things, but this was more than deeply personal, it was traumatic. And his refusal to explain how he saw her still hurt—

I could give you things you would never otherwise have had.

Yes. Indescribable heartbreak being one of them.

Too hot and bothered to stay in bed, she yanked on her bikini, went to the studio and lost herself in playing in the treasure trove of the supplies. A couple of hours drifted by, but then she heard splashing. Glancing out once was too much. Ares was a vision with the sun beating down on his perfect frame as he swam from one end to the other over and over. For the next hour she tried not to watch. Tired, cranky and conflicted, she wanted to dive in too except he was still in the pool and every few minutes she caught another glimpse. The last thing she needed was to get close to him almost naked. Again. She was having a hard enough time concentrating as it was.

Yesterday he'd walked away from her the instant she'd refused him, but he'd not been entirely wrong. He wasn't alone in wanting; she yearned for the intensely fulfilling physicality he could deliver. But that encounter in his office had been emotionally fraught. She couldn't endure his rejection if he stopped again. So she would remain wise and in control and away from him. But knowing more now—not seeing him through the rose-coloured glasses of naïve youth—had her questioning everything. She felt jittery, as if she'd had too much coffee when she'd actually had none. She needed a break.

She bypassed the pool to walk through the villa. Memories followed her like wraiths, demanding attention she refused to give. She went to the storeroom just off the kitchen, knowing it was stocked with extra supplies. She would load a box to keep in the studio so she didn't have to come back into the main villa too often.

There were bottles of *lemonada* in massive supply and she fossicked about for salty snacks to nibble on and match her mood. That was when she caught a glimpse of blue. She paused. Stared. Pushed to the back of a shelf, it was mostly hidden by a stack of boxes. With a jerky shove she toppled the box tower so she could reach it quickly. If she'd been angry before, she was furious now. She totally forgot about drinks and snacks. It took two hands to lift. She remembered the weight of it. Her thumb slipped into the perfect indentation she'd made near the base. Carrying it out, she passed a small cubby stocked with a few hardware tools. One was *exactly* what she needed. She tucked it under her arm and with ice-cold determination carried both the sculpture and the hammer out to the pool where Ares was still swimming lap after infuriating lap.

She set the piece on a table in the shade. It was the table where their post-wedding champagne and canapés had been placed that picturesque day. She stepped back and studied it with frigid clarity. The multi-media work, with its fine glazed clay imprinted by snippets of hand-pulled lace, shells, sea glass and rope she'd knotted, was a mirror for the blues of the pool and sea and sky. She'd put *hours* into it. But in the end she'd not been able to keep it because too much of her soul had been poured into it. It had been a cathartic expression of her love for this place and the experiences she'd had here. She'd released just some of that emotion into the combination of lace and clay and light. Before making this piece she'd not considered herself an artist—

Raw fury energised her. She hefted the hammer, tested the weight, working out how to get maximum impact. Holding it in both hands, she swung it back. Just as it arced over her head, harsh hands gripped her—locking her painfully in place. Next second the hammer was ripped from her grip.

'What the *hell* are you doing?' Ares yelled, releasing one arm and wrenching the other down, spinning her to face him.

She heard a thud. He'd tossed the hammer into the garden.

'Why would you want to do that?' Applying more pressure on her wrist, he drew her back from the table and closer to him.

Water dripped from him, splashing droplets on her.

Muscles gleaming. Eyes ablaze. His black trunks clung, moulding to his strong thighs. But she wasn't looking at his body. She was enraged by his *treachery*.

'Why do you have it?' Because she still couldn't believe what was right in front of her. 'You bought it from that art auction, right?'

Still looking shocked, he pressed a hand to her forehead then tugged her further out of the sun. 'You're hot. Are you not well?'

'Why?' she yelled.

His hold gentled but he still didn't release her. 'Why does my having it bother you?'

Because she'd thought someone—some random *stranger*—had appreciated her work. Someone she didn't know and who didn't know her. Someone who had simply seen her piece and been moved by it enough to *want* it. That happening had allowed her to believe she might have a future, not just in her props design, but in *art*. But that wasn't what had happened at all. Ares Vasiliadis had made a mockery of her dreams. Again.

'Why did you buy it?' she repeated, struggling to regain some kind of control.

How had he even known it was for sale? So much for only knowing where she lived and worked. He'd known more. And now it hit her—he hadn't come for her but he'd wanted to give her money. This had been a *charity* purchase. The independence that she'd thought she was building was a facade. She felt so stupid all over again. Because of him.

'I thought I made it clear I didn't want anything from you,' she railed. 'Certainly not your money.'

'I didn't buy it as a way of getting money to you.' He

wiped water from his forehead with his free hand. 'I honestly didn't think that deeply about it.'

'So it was an impulse purchase?' she tossed at him, even more hurt. 'Much like our marriage in the first place.'

'Why is this such a big deal?' He glared at her. 'What does it matter?'

'Because I thought it went into the atrium of some business. That people might actually see it. Might appreciate it. Instead it's shut away in some poky cupboard on an island no one comes to. It might as well not exist, for all the joy it brings.' Barely seen, barely appreciated and not fulfilling its purpose at all. 'Which is what you wanted to do with me too, right? Shove me here—'

'Because I thought you loved it here!' he exploded. 'I thought this was the place of your dreams. Isn't that what you said? You *told* me there was nowhere else you *ever* wanted to be!'

Because *he* was here too—*that* was what she'd meant. She'd never wanted her husband to live apart from her more than half the time. She'd wanted to be with him—would have followed him wherever he'd wanted to go. Instead she would have been like this—an unvalued trophy gathering dust.

'Why would you break it?' he asked. 'It's mine. I'm not going to let you destroy it.'

'What do you like about it, then?' she challenged. She'd told him why it mattered to her, now it was his turn. But he was silent.

'What was it that spoke to you?' she prompted. 'Why did you have to have it so badly that you paid far more than it ever cost to make?'

Asking what something meant to him had been a question he'd not been able to answer before, but that wasn't good enough—he had to answer her this time.

He stared at her. Hard. But his voice was soft. 'It was worth it to me.'

'Why?' She knew he could feel her shaking.

His gaze shifted from her to the table. A few moments passed before he drew breath. Bethan steeled her heart.

'It reminded me of here,' he murmured. 'I liked the lacework. The whirls from the shells.' He pointed to a low spot of the vessel. 'That blue is the exact blue of the water down by the boat shed.'

And of his eyes. She felt his fingers shift on her wrist.

'I liked the form,' he added, pointing to another part. 'This washes like the wave over that split rock on the beach, this mirrors that branch of that olive tree.'

She blinked to hold back her spiralling emotion because he'd nailed it. He'd seen it exactly as she'd seen it in her mind. He'd *understood*. And now she couldn't actually speak. He looked at her, a new storm building in his eyes.

'It *was* in the office,' he said savagely. 'In Athens. Not in reception but in *my* office upstairs. It was there until I couldn't stand to look at it any more.'

'Why couldn't you stand to look at it any more?' she whispered.

'Do you really need to ask? Can you honestly not work it out?' he erupted. 'It *hurt*, Bethan. You hurt.' He dragged in a breath. 'You hurt me.'

He finally released her and stalked towards the villa but only got two paces before she grabbed his arm as hard as he'd gripped hers.

'You can't say that and then just walk away.'

'Why not?' he snapped back and stepped towards her. 'Isn't that what you did?'

She paused. The truth hit hard. She'd done exactly that. 'Maybe I shouldn't have.'

The wildness in him ignited and he grabbed her waist, tugging her against him. 'It's too late to say that.'

Yes. They were on the verge of divorce. But now she felt his hard, hot sun-dried body pressing insistently against her. Felt his biceps bunch beneath her grip and his hold on her tighten.

'It's far too late,' he repeated in a whisper.

Emotion surged. She knew that look in his eyes. She knew *exactly*. 'It is. *Yes*.'

His hands hit her waist and hauled her close while she reached around his neck to bring him closer still. Her breasts smashed against his hard chest. Sensation shot from her too-sensitive nipples to where she was slick and hot.

'But there's still this,' he raged.

There would *always* be this. That was her true fear—that she would never shake free of it.

'*This* is what needs to be destroyed,' she growled. 'I want you to destroy it with me.'

His hands swept lower to her butt and he hoisted her. She instantly wrapped her legs around his waist, shuddering as her pelvis pressed against his. He stalked, not to her room, but to his. It was a dark cave-like space with navy sheets on the enormous bed and no other furniture. He tossed her with such energy she bounced over the mattress. With a savage laugh he grabbed her ankle and slid her back to him. He stripped her in seconds. His savage intensity turned her on more. He wanted her ruin as much as she wanted his. But he didn't tumble down to the sheets with her. Instead he stepped back and surveyed her—naked and sprawled on his bed. The smile on his face was utterly predatory.

'It's not going to be fast, Bethan. And you're staying right here until we're done.'

As angry, as aroused, as she was, his expression caught her fast. Almost paralysed with need, she shivered as he skimmed light strokes down her body. She was so turned on it would take nothing.

'Such bounty,' he drawled. 'So sensitive.'

Oh, she was. He cupped her breasts but even in his big hands her flesh overflowed. His thumbs scraped over her tight buds. She arched her hips. He wasn't even touching her sex but she was so close to coming.

'Ares...'

He kept tormenting her nipples with that feral smile as she twisted beneath him. So close. So *close*. But just as she arched—the jerk didn't let her finish. He chuckled and moved his attentions away. She gasped and he merely kissed her with an almost mean lightness as the release slipped beyond her reach. She breathed hard, glaring at him as he sat back and watched her anger ignite.

'Ares.'

He ignored her stare, dropping his focus to her legs. He palmed her thighs, spreading them. Relief swept through her. Briefly. Because once again he teased—so lightly, so consistently—until once more she strained. Almost there. *Almost*. And once more he released her. Eased her back from the precipice with deliberately slow caresses going in the wrong damned direction. And she was going to kill him. After she came. Desperately she slipped her fingers between her legs but he gripped her wrist and yanked it away.

'Oh, you don't get to do that,' he scolded. 'You come when I let you.'

'Controlling bastard,' she muttered.

'That's exactly right.'

'You'll pay.'

'Looking forward to taking it from you later, but right now it's my turn.' He silenced her with his mouth.

She writhed, levering herself to rub against him however she could, frantic to cross that finish line. The second he lifted his lips to catch breath she just begged. Again.

He looked down at her for a long moment as something like despair shadowed his eyes. 'I cannot fucking resist you.'

He slid down her body, burying his face and fingers in her.

The scream ripped from her throat as he wrung the most intense orgasm of her life from her. Even then he didn't ease up. Didn't release her from the shuddering sensations until she was basically levitating off the bed.

Everything went black. By the time she opened her eyes he was standing beside her. Naked. Cock sheathed and straining.

She moaned, her sex dripping at the sight of him—all the exhaustion of her orgasm instantly replaced by an intense ache. 'Please, Ares.'

He looked down on her. Anger and satisfaction in his eyes. 'You want me?'

'You know I do.'

'Tell me.'

She had already. So many times. 'Needy jerk.'

'For you? Absolutely.' He moved onto the bed. 'Tell me how hungry you are for me.'

'You can feel it for yourself already.' She was strung out and shaking.

'I can,' he grunted. 'I can taste it. I'm going to tease you to orgasm again and again. I'm going to make you come until you can't stand it any more and you're begging me to stop.' He rose and planted himself over her. 'And then I'm going to make you come again.'

With unbridled anger and passion he kissed her, dropping his body to press her to the bed.

'Please,' she moaned. 'Please, please, please.' She rocked her hips desperately, wanting him more than ever.

'We will *end* this,' he growled ruthlessly.

He really wanted rid of this? Well, so did she.

'Then hurry up and try,' she taunted.

His pupils were so blown it looked as if his eyes were black. He plastered over her. Pinning her in place. Bethan breathed in sharply. He was bigger than she remembered and though she was wet and pleasured, he was still...*something*. She bit back the revelation that it had been so very long. That didn't matter. Nothing mattered but right *now*.

She saw the strain in his eyes as he stared—watching her reactions—his breath hissing between his clenched teeth as he finally pushed inside her. And that was all it took.

She erupted about him, rocked by another intense release. But he braced—utterly still.

'This is not going to be over that quickly,' he roared.

Oh, it was far too late for her. She laughed, exultant in her ecstasy.

'No?' She pressed her nails down his spine and into the tight curve of his buttocks.

He stiffened. *'Bethan.'*

'Take me harder.'

He didn't thrust into her. He slammed with his full force. His hands tightened, holding her so there was no escape. Not that she ever wanted one. She groaned, revelling in the wildness of his passion. This was physical and fierce. Purely about the release—the burn of their damned endless chemistry. And again it hit—quick.

She couldn't speak. Couldn't catch her breath. He was still pressing her into the mattress but somehow his hold felt gentler—as if he was cradling her. She never wanted to move on from this moment. Certainly didn't want to consider what it meant—it had to be nothing.

Groaning, he finally rolled to his side, releasing her so she could breathe. But she'd liked the weight of him on her. It had anchored her after such raw physicality. But now coolness came between them.

'I didn't think it was possible for us to surpass ourselves,' he muttered. 'But we just did.'

Sex. Just sex. That was all this had ever really been. The thought skinned her already bruised heart. But worse, she was hot inside all over again. How was that even possible? *Somehow* they had to end this. She turned to him—registered the smouldering need rebuilding in his eyes—knew hers reflected the same.

'Try again.'

CHAPTER SEVEN

ARES SHOULDN'T HAVE been able to so much as lift his pinkie finger for at least another four hours but his pulse was erratic and, despite his muscular exhaustion, his mind raced, making sleep elusive. Worse, *need* clawed low—cancelling all remaining capacity to rest. Bethan, however, was fast asleep, her hair a tangled river across the pillow.

He rose, quelling his rampaging inner reaction long enough to take in the light abrasions on her mouth from his stubble and the two faint blemishes appearing on her arm. There were a couple developing on him too. Neither of them had been particularly gentle. He covered her exposed limbs with the soft sheet, rejecting the tormenting temptation to wake her with a kiss. It had been so much better than he'd remembered, than he'd fantasised, than he could believe. It was devastating. As was the fact he was *still* ravenous. That singularly basic experience had only served to reveal the infinite crevasse that was his need. But it wouldn't be the same for her—she'd dated during their separation so that wouldn't have been her first time in forever. Wouldn't have been as shattering. But it looked as if she would sleep for a century.

He turned away. He didn't want to think about any men she'd dated. Couldn't stomach the jealousy filling him. It was wretched that he'd not felt this *good* in so long. How could he be this in thrall to her still?

He rubbed his chest, soothing his stuttering pulse, and walked to the farthest bathroom. But the current unevenness of his heartbeat was different from the palpitations that had landed him in a sterile room with a plethora of sensors and wires stuck to him. Even so, he practised his damned breathing as he stood beneath a cold shower and tried to haul his wits together. Only the horrifying moment he'd caught her about to shatter her sculpture replayed in his mind. Her anger both awed and appalled him. How could she consider smashing something that had taken so much to make—not only skill, but *soul*. It tore *his* heart that she'd wanted to destroy it. But she'd wanted to destroy the chemistry that still bound them together too. As did he. And they had just then, no? Maybe now they could both move on with their lives.

He dressed and went out to the pool. He'd not been back here since he'd been released from that two-day hospital stint. He'd wanted to remain out of sight and keep any rumours of a condition quiet from the company—and his family—while he followed doctor's orders and 'relaxed'. In fact, he'd done a full reset. He'd had an epiphany about his future—what he wanted to do and how. Finalising the divorce had been high up there. He'd truly thought they were over. Apparently they weren't.

Unlike his family and basically the rest of the world, Bethan hadn't wanted much from him other than his body. It was all she wanted still. And why was he angry with her about that when all he wanted was hers too? Because she *had* wanted more. She'd wanted the heart he didn't have. And now she didn't. Now the sweet, warm, eagerly loving wife he'd married was irrevocably altered. She didn't shyly admit eager, hot things that made him lose his head any more. She'd been a little irresistible marshmallow—sweet, soft, delicious—and he'd been able to read her easily. Or he'd thought he'd been able to. But her deep wishes hadn't been as obvious as they'd appeared. Now she had claws, a spine, pride. More than that, she had a brittle veneer of cynicism. That was his fault. He missed her emotional vulnerability even though now, while guarded, she spoke with brutal honesty.

He picked up the sculpture. He'd meant everything he'd said about it. He got so lost in looking at it, he'd had to hide it. But yeah, it never should've been put on that shelf. She thought he wanted to keep *her* hidden. That he was ashamed of her when nothing could be further from the truth. He'd wanted to *protect* her—from his family, no? Only stupidly he'd never explained that. And not only his family. Guilt niggled. *He'd* wanted to maintain some distance from her. Compartmentalise the business and the personal in his life. Grimacing, he carried her piece into the lounge.

Bethan was standing there watching him. She couldn't have been deeply asleep at all, given she'd showered. Both her trousers and plain white tee clung to her body and made her look like a 1950s screen siren. She fiddled with the slim gold bangle she always wore. He paused just inside the threshold trying to read her shadowed eyes and not react too explicitly—he couldn't pounce on her again when that had been so fierce and raw and... still *unfinished*.

He cleared his throat. 'Are you okay?'

She nodded towards the sculpture. 'What are you going to do with it?'

'Put it somewhere safe.' He reached for an easy tone. 'I paid a lot of money for it.'

He walked past her to set it on the shelf at the back of the room—away from sun damage but able to be seen. Needing distraction, he rubbed the back of his neck, made himself sit in one of the large armchairs and dredged up conversation. 'When did you make the leap from making props to sculpture?'

She sat in another seat. The polite distance felt ridiculous given they'd passionately stripped each other less than an hour ago.

'You didn't read the "about the artist" paragraph from the auction house?' she replied.

There it was—that new little bite. He wasn't going to overreact. He'd just answer.

'I saw it because of an Internet alert I had on your name.' He was unapologetic about that. He'd needed to keep a search running in case of reputational damage. The alert had pinged, he'd clicked the link and madness had overtaken him. He'd have paid anything to own it. 'It said you were a props designer branching into custom art pieces. That you were a new and exciting artist with jaw-dropping skill. I know you were making things long before then—you were making things when you were on holiday with me, that's why I built the studio for you, but your work then wasn't like that—' He paused, remembering her sitting cross-legged crafting in the shade. One day she'd spotted lacework at the local village and he'd arranged for her to meet the maker. She'd spent hours with the woman, fascinated. She'd picked it up quickly and he'd been fascinated watching her. 'Not so...' he shrugged '...complete.'

Bethan sank further into the large armchair—simply unable to get up and walk away even when she should. Too touched by the fact that he could quote part of the blurb from the auction house. That he'd seen her crafting—but of course he had, it was why he'd created that studio. Ares noticed a lot and perhaps she'd been the one not to notice some things as they actually were. His defences for one thing. His calm, arrogant facade in certain situations like the event they'd inadvertently gate-crashed at his headquarters. Like the fact he'd revealed so little about his complex family for so long and been so matter of fact about an arrangement she found quite shocking. But she'd never seen him as emotional as when he'd stopped her from smashing her sculpture. His mask was mostly back now. He was wary. So was she. Her skin—her heart—felt flayed. That sex hadn't eased anything. She ached more, utterly exposed and emotionally strung out, too uncertain about where they now stood, so she grasped the 'safe topic' olive branch he'd just offered.

'I met Elodie in my first week in London. I'd signed with a temp cleaning agency and was sent to the escape room company she managed.'

'I would have helped you with money, Bethan,' he muttered. 'Was the thought of asking me so awful?'

'Why should you have to? We made a mistake—'

'You didn't need to *hide* from me.'

So much for a safe topic. She bowed her head, trying to hold it together because it felt important to explain. 'I guess I wanted to be independent. I needed to know I could be.'

She'd wanted to start over. To know she could survive—*alone*. Because she *was* alone—she'd lost all her family. Maybe she'd rushed it with Ares because she'd been grieving and lonely and so she'd flung herself into a bubble of romance. It wasn't real, of course it had burst and she'd needed to just…carry on and make it through herself as she should have before him.

'Elodie and I got on well,' she said. Elodie had taken one look at her and taken her under her wing. 'She gave me a permanent position. I noticed some of the props were damaged and quietly fixed them. Elodie asked if I could make some from scratch and soon I wasn't cleaning any more but was full-time making props and helping create whole rooms.'

She'd loved the creative challenge and the more she'd done, the more her creativity had fired.

'Through Elodie, I met Phoebe. She needed a flatmate and I needed a more permanent place to stay. They're good friends.'

They were loyal and supportive and respectful of the boundaries Bethan had needed—the slightest of distances to keep her shredded heart safe.

'I'm glad you found them,' he said huskily. 'But you didn't just suddenly acquire all those skills. I know your grandmother taught you some, but you work with ceramics, you solder, you make complex mechanisms for secret boxes to hide clues. You can make magical things out of almost nothing. How did you learn it all?'

She studied the bangle she'd been absently opening and closing for the last ten minutes. 'This was my mother's. It's one of the few things I have of hers. She and my dad met when he went into the cafe she was working at.'

'You said he was a navy man.' He nodded.

'Right. A maritime engineer. It was pretty quick. They were really happy. I've seen the photos. My grandmother told me the story of how they met so many times.'

They'd had a *once in a lifetime* love. Her grandmother had experienced one of those too. So Bethan had assumed such miracles were normal.

'Anyway, when I was a toddler Dad was away on an exercise for a couple of months. Mum was pregnant again—almost at term and she was really tired. My dad's mother came and took me up to her place in Scotland to give her a break. But that night my mother left an element on by accident. She and the baby didn't survive the fire.'

'Bethan—'

'I know,' she nodded, appreciating the horror in his eyes. 'It was terrible for my father but he had to work and that took him away a lot. So I never left Scotland. Dad sold our house in Wales and moved back in with his mother and me. My grandmother had been widowed too—lost the love of her life ten years earlier, so she understood Dad's grief. Honestly, after that my childhood was idyllic. It was a small, lovely village and our cottage was cosy. It was filled with photos and trinkets—so many fond memories of my mother and my grandfather.

Never a day passed without mention of them, the stories of how my mum and dad met. They were lost but never gone, you know? Dad adored me and I loved him and when he was home on leave, we'd work in his father's shed. He'd teach me so many things like—'

'Soldering mechanisms.' Ares nodded.

'Yes, and all the rope knots.'

'But something wasn't right.' Ares frowned.

Yeah, he was astute. 'There was an exclusive boarding school down the road that cost a lot of money. Dad worked so hard to send me there as a day student so I didn't have to leave home and I never wanted him to think I was ungrateful.'

'You were unhappy there.'

Desperately so. 'They were real rich bitch types, you know? I wasn't from wealth like that.'

'They made you feel inferior?'

'I didn't fit in and we all knew it. I stayed in the library at lunchtime, stayed offline, tried to stay invisible.'

'You could never be invisible.'

'Yeah. I guess so because they still got to me.'

His jaw tightened.

'Not physically or anything really bad. Just endless cutting comments,' she said quietly. 'They mocked my lack of properties—that there were no holidays abroad. They had no idea that I loved going out in a skiff with Dad and just being home with him. They teased my big body, my uncool clothes. My old-fashioned hobbies. Apparently I was like a grandma, which wasn't an insult to me at all. And when my grandmother got sick in my last year, I dropped out.' She'd been happy to.

'Your dad didn't come back when she got sick?'

'At first. But she was sick for a while and we needed money and he had to go back. I was there, I didn't need anyone else to help when she'd done so much for me.'

'And by being busy with her, you could avoid living your life. Avoid interacting with people your own age who'd been horrible,' he suggested softly. 'It was safe.'

'I loved her. I *wanted* to be the one to take care of her.' Anger rippled. *She* wasn't the one who avoided people.

'I know. But still...' He angled his head and challenged her with those all-seeing eyes. 'Sometimes there can be more than one reason why we do things, no? We tell ourselves we're doing something for someone else's benefit but also...really...it sometimes has selfish elements.'

'You're saying our choices can be multilayered. Because life is complicated.' She knew what he was getting at really.

His choice to marry her. *When* he had. *How* he had.

Maybe he was right again. Now she knew there was more to that decision than she'd understood because she'd been blinded by her own privileges. She'd grown up in a loving family, but she'd been ignorant. The lessons she'd learned about love from her adoring family were honestly too good to be true. Too easy. She'd barely had *half* a picture.

Ares frowned again. 'What happened to your dad?'

She opened the clasp once more. 'He died three months after I'd finished school. There was a landslide caused by a flash flood. He was digging out a person who was trapped when there was another big slip.'

For such a lithe, fit man Ares could sit surprisingly still. It was a change—he'd always been active before.

Now she watched his even breathing. It was too even. Was he *counting*? Using a relaxation strategy because he was stressed?

It wasn't that he really *cared*, he was just empathetic, right? Because he'd lost his parents too. They had more in common than she'd realised. And she needed to explain her part in why they hadn't worked. Because it would help with this. The *end*. And it was easier to talk about her past than deal with the fragile emotions of the present.

'After my grandmother died I had to sell our home to pay off the debt we'd gotten into. The little left over paid for my trip to Greece. She knew I'd always wanted to come here and made me promise that I'd do it. For her—for my father too. I know I told you that she'd died, but not that it was only two months before I got here.'

Ares's eye widened. 'She was sick for *years*.'

Bethan nodded. She'd stayed in the cottage. 'I crafted in the evenings, banged about in my grandfather's shed during the day when she was resting. It was quiet but I wasn't lonely. I didn't tell you because I didn't want to bring the mood down, you know?' She sent him a soft, sad smile. 'I was having so much fun with you but the truth is I was grieving and it was an escape.'

Perhaps for them both. Perhaps he too had wanted to forget reality—the pressure of being Ares Vasiliadis. It had just been a few weeks of all the good things and only the good things. It had been *her* mistake in thinking that perfection could last forever.

'I owe you an apology,' she said with sudden clarity. 'I was needy. And I was so naïve. I'm sorry about that.'

His gaze lifted, shocked. 'What?'

'Ares, I was inexperienced in a lot of things, but especially the realities of a relationship.' She turned to him earnestly. 'It's taken me an age to realise I only heard *stories* of perfect marriages. I never saw any actually *work*. I never witnessed the normal ups and downs, no working through issues or anything. I was repeatedly *told* about my parents' once-in-a-lifetime love—and that of my grandparents—but I was only told the *good* bits, right? So I naïvely believed there were *only* good bits. That if you'd met the "one" then everything was miraculously easy. I put all that expectation on *you*. It was an impossible burden. Especially when you really had no idea how lonely I'd been, how ill-equipped I was to speak up or even compromise.

'It wasn't fair of me to expect that you'd fill all my emotional gaps—and there were plenty. The first moment things got tricky, I didn't know how to fix it.' How to fight for what she'd truly wanted. 'I was insecure. I'd thought you were a ferryman—a sailor, like Dad. I could relate to that and I thought we were a match. I could live with this villa—but when we went to Athens I learned there were more properties and planes and all kinds of expectations. That compound was so cold and so was everyone in it.' And he'd turned cold too. He'd turned to stone. 'You were in another *realm* from me. I got scared. I took Gia's words as gospel. I used those Sophia stories as part of my reason to run, but it was a release for you too.'

He stiffened.

'You know I'm right,' she said softly.

But even now she couldn't bring herself to remind

him of his refusal to answer the one question she'd been brave enough to ask. His inability to say he loved her.

'You know I don't fit into that world,' she finished.

'I never was ashamed of you,' he said huskily.

She paused. He'd said that yesterday and she wanted to believe him but—

'I didn't want to hide you here,' he added. 'I truly didn't think you wanted to live in a big city.'

'I've spent the last two and a bit years living in London,' she pointed out wryly.

'But you liked the small town you grew up in in Scotland. You told me that back then,' he said fiercely.

She glanced up. He'd really paid attention to what little she had said about her past?

'You said that being on this island was like that only with better weather, better food,' he added. 'You stood in this room and said you never wanted to leave. Ever.'

She'd never wanted to leave *him*. She would have followed him to the ends of the earth. But he was right—he'd just quoted her perfectly.

'Was that a lie?' he asked eventually.

'No. I just... I hadn't really meant it like that because it wasn't a real possibility. I would've needed a job...'

But now—far too late—she realised that for him it was *entirely* possible. It would have been nothing for him to keep her here. He had the money to make it all happen. He'd taken her fantasy wish at face value because for him it *wasn't* an impossible dream but easily achievable.

'I knew you'd need occupation so I had the studio fitted out,' he murmured. 'I'd hoped to make you happy.'

His self-mocking smile hurt her heart.

'Which would have been an impossibility,' she said softly.

Maybe he'd not been ashamed of her. Maybe his avoidance of Athens—of mentioning his family—hadn't been about her at all, but his *own* issue—shame or pain or something that she still didn't know about.

'*No one* could live up to my naïve relationship ideals back then,' she murmured sadly. 'Certainly not someone…'

'Like me?' He frowned.

'Hurt,' she breathed. 'Hurt, like you.'

His expression went more mask-like than ever. She'd not meant to put this on him. She'd meant to own *her* part in it, not air her new assumptions about him. But here she was, talking too much.

'I don't mean by me,' she muttered with a self-mocking smile of her own. 'You don't have to tell me why, but I know there's a wall you retreat behind. I think it's been there since before we met and I'm sure you had good reasons to build it.'

She paused again, heart thundering. This was a risk but she wanted to clear the air properly. Then maybe they could put this behind them. And she'd meant it. He didn't have to explain if he didn't want to…

And clearly he didn't. Because he was silent for too many beats for her stressed brain to count.

'You never would have been a burden,' he rasped. 'Not to me.'

His eventual raw reply smote her heart. She waited but he didn't say anything more. Didn't deny what she'd said nor explain. He was definitely hurt and his defences—barriers—were back up. Masking pain and not allowing more. And wasn't that fair enough? Because *that* was the mistake they'd made—thinking they shared more than a physical connection. There hadn't been a truly emotional one and there still wasn't. His silence *now* reinforced that. And that had to be okay, because she wasn't naïve any more. Life was never a fairy tale. She could survive this.

'I'm going to grab a tonne of the food that's in the fridge.' She stood, hiding her shattered insides. Sometimes comfort eating was the only way. 'I'm going to eat it while watching a movie.' She cocked her head and tried to be rational and adult and mature. 'You want to join me?'

CHAPTER EIGHT

ARES GRAZED ON the popcorn with a continuous, smooth movement of his hand—bowl to mouth to bowl to mouth—stuffing the gaping wound she'd ripped the scab from, stopping himself from speaking. But it didn't stop him from *thinking*. He hated that she'd felt the need to apologise for being sweet and young and romantic. For having dreams. And he hated that she was right. He'd been hurt. Before her. Yes, he had some walls. And he was keeping them. And because of that, he couldn't touch her again. It wouldn't be fair.

She'd chosen the first of a street-racing movie franchise with ten instalments. Muscle cars, muscle men, explosions, high-speed chases. Bethan's wide eyes made him chuckle. She was knitting—her nimble hands never, ever still. The new piece was quickly taking shape. Soft pastels in a pretty pattern. He realised it was a baby's jumper. Was it a gift? Had to be. But his brain tortured him with the vision of Bethan cradling *her* baby. Then teaching her toddler all her skills. She would have been a nymph here, spending her time swimming and sailing with a cherub or two in tow. Idyllic, no? The few magical days he'd had as a child with his mother on the beach could have been an *everyday* joy for his child—with Bethan. Not him. She was the loving one.

But he would have provided for them. He would have given her everything he could. Nanny. Chef. Housekeeper. The space to unleash her creativity and craft. But she wanted *more*.

'Who is it for?' he asked huskily when she glanced up and caught him staring.

'My friend Phoebe is pregnant,' she said.

'It's beautiful.' He kept his popcorn fingers far away from the fine wool.

She blushed and bent her head, her face an open book again. He just knew that for a second there she'd thought about having a child too. When he'd met her he'd thought she'd been sweet and guileless and inexperienced but she'd not been entirely so—not in one fundamental way. She'd known love but she'd known such *loss* too. Both her parents. A sibling mere weeks from being born—she'd lost that relationship before it had even begun. He knew the ache of that—the loss of all the *possibility*, the banter and fun to be had with your brother or sister. And then she'd lost her grandmother of course—in a long, slow sickness. There was so much grief in her, he didn't know how she still smiled so readily.

And she'd been bullied by snobby classmates. That anyone could be cruel to someone gentle and creative and kind enraged him. That they'd made her feel inferior. But his actions, his family, had echoed that hurt in her—she'd thought she was not good enough for them? She was far *too* good. She wanted a full, happy family and she *should* have that in her future.

But back then she'd been wounded and wary—actually as careful of her heart as he. He'd known loss too. And rejection. From family, not from school friends. His father. His mother. He'd known failure. So their reasons differed, but they'd each chosen not to reveal too much. He'd hidden parts of himself. Like her, he'd been too busy having fun—too busy seducing her. Why would he ever revisit his own personal hell? Why ever share that with her?

Now he thought about all the things she'd said and the things he'd left *un*said. He would leave them unspoken. There was no need, no point, to talk. She'd built a life in London. Made her friends. Found her career. Started dating. She was flourishing and happy *without* him. They just had the one thing left. The one thing it had always come down to. One kernel of pure chemistry. But he'd ignored it for more than two years. He could ignore it for a few days more. Because this afternoon—that frantic, physical encounter—had been wild and devastating and in no way had destroyed the magnetism that drew them together. But it wasn't fair to do that again when he had no intention—ability, even—of opening up to her in the way she had with him. The honesty he owed her was an impossible ask.

The second film in the franchise started and he sank lower into the sofa. By the time the credits began for the third he realised her hands were still. She'd fallen asleep. He carefully extracted the soft wool from her lap and placed it safely on the table. Then he lifted her into his arms. She stirred. He shushed.

'Go back to sleep,' he whispered.

For once she didn't argue with him. Those beautiful eyes remained closed. He carried her to the bed they'd shared for those first magical nights, tucked her in, turned away before temptation could control him.

They wanted *different* things. The love she wanted from him wasn't a kind he could offer. He didn't feel it, didn't believe in it. He wasn't just 'hurt', he was irreparably damaged. The broken bastard, the unwanted son of Loukas Vasiliadis. Shame and anger bubbled within because he knew—to his bones—that he was unwanted still. It was only his skill, only the power he'd fought so long to attain, that kept him in that damned company. If he'd failed there they would have cast him out.

The next morning he worked in the study for as long as he could—which wasn't nearly long enough. When he walked out she was in the pool. He watched briefly then turned. The memories here were too strong—blurring past and present and confusing him. While his anger with her had eased, the lust hadn't. If he were a better man he would take her back to Athens now, organise the notary and get the divorce settled. But there were only a few more days until the foundation gala and he wanted her there. He wasn't great at talking and he couldn't help wondering weakly if she might even want to attend of her own volition. Maybe he could *show* her what he was doing—why it mattered. She'd been brave enough to be honest with him, surely he could manage the same to a degree. Because that truth was coming out anyway—it was a huge part of his goal. So why not tell her now?

But he still wouldn't touch her again. Wouldn't mess this up when they'd made progress towards a peaceable closure. He went back to the study, made a couple of calls, then went down to the beach to prepare. Two hours later he hunted her down in the studio that had lain dormant for so long and now was vibrant.

'Want to come out on the water with me?' He glanced about, avoiding taking in how lush she looked with flushed cheeks and a smear of paint on her cheek.

She'd made the room hers so quickly. Occupied it only a few hours yet it was infused with vitality and creativity. Okay, mess. But he liked the colour and chaos.

'Now?' She cleared her throat. 'Okay, let me just clean up.'

She didn't ask where they were going, not even when they stepped onto the boat and he started the engine. She just ran her hand through her hair and turned her face to the breeze. He knew her love of the water came from those hours with her father. That she felt at home on the waves. He did too, thanks to his mother. Those carefree times had been so special.

It was half an hour before he rounded the coastline and *Artemis* came into view. The stunning yacht was anchored in a cove, one of the jewels in the luxury yacht arm of the Vasiliadis empire.

'Are we going onboard *that*?' Bethan asked as they pulled alongside her.

Ares pulled her bag from the stow and tossed it up to a waiting deckhand, chuckling at her astonished gaze. 'Don't worry, I remembered your knitting.'

'How long are we staying?'

'Just a couple of nights. We'll make our way back to Athens this way, okay?'

'Oh. Great.' But something flickered in her eyes before she looked away.

She nimbly stepped from the small boat to what his crew joked was the 'mother ship'. The crew lined up to greet them, then the bosun and one of the deckhands returned the small motorboat to its mooring and used a jet ski to get back. Ares followed Bethan as Carina, the trainee steward, took her on a tour of the boat. He saw Bethan's eyes widen at the large jacuzzi and suppressed his damned thoughts. Then Carina took them below and showed them the rooms. Bethan's adjoined his. But, he reminded himself, the doors did lock.

Bethan was nothing but effusive. 'This is stunning,' she said to the steward. 'I'm too scared to touch anything, it's so perfectly polished.'

'I'll leave you to settle in.' The steward smiled shyly. 'We'll have drinks on deck for whenever you're ready.'

'Thank you, Carina,' Ares said.

He closed the door after Carina, crossed his arms and smirked, knowing that look in Bethan's eyes. 'What do you think?'

'I think a crew of *twenty* to serve only two is somewhat extravagant,' she said, fidgeting with her bangle and studiously not looking at the large bed just beside her. 'And some of them seem pretty young.'

Right.

'It's a big boat, takes a few to keep it running.' He

cocked his head and chuckled. 'Would you prefer a smaller boat so we can stay in even closer quarters?'

'Actually, about that, perhaps I might move to another—'

'Sorry, not possible.' He'd already inquired. 'The crew are in the other cabins.'

Her eyebrows arched. 'You let crew use the guest cabins?'

'Those young ones you spotted are trainees. That's why there are so many. They need to understand the complete guest experience in order to be able to provide it. To know what luxury service feels like.'

'You let *trainees* loose on a boat like this?'

He nodded, curious to see her reaction. 'Young people ought to be able to thrive in the industry. Kids from disadvantaged backgrounds deserve good training and experience to develop their talent. They should know their rights and have the support to rise through the ranks as well as anyone.'

It was a main goal of the Melina Foundation. After that health scare he wanted a legacy he could feel good about and this was a way of bringing his mother's name into the light. The smallest of reparations he could make to her.

'I had no idea you did this.' Her gaze warmed.

Of course she hadn't. And he shouldn't have started this conversation in such an intimate room. 'Come on, let's go get that drink and find out where they're going to take us on the way to Athens.'

'You've not instructed them on the route?'

'I'm testing their creativity.' He chuckled. 'As I said, it's a training trip.'

Bethan clearly took the fact they were trainees to heart. She offered nothing but enthusiastic support to the two stewards on deck—effusive in her appreciation of the welcome cocktail they'd prepared. Then she paced to the bow of the boat, her eyes sparkling as she explored it alone. He watched her lean over the railing to stare into the water. The breeze restored colour to her cheeks and a sparkle to her eye. She looked like a curvaceous mermaid. Water—swimming, diving, sailing—had always been her happy place. And this had been a good idea.

Bethan inhaled the salty air, suppressing her heartache about leaving the villa. No doubt Ares would have the rest of her things packed up and shipped over, but, like the last time she'd left for Athens, she'd not realised she wouldn't return there. Impossibly, this time it felt more devastating because she knew for certain she wouldn't ever go back.

They were almost over. Since that searing—utterly ruinous—time together yesterday, he'd not attempted to touch her. She vaguely remembered him carrying her to bed last night, but he'd not gotten in with her. She'd had to swim first thing to ease the yearning aches in her body and cool her simmering heat. To hide the bruise deepening on her heart. Here and now he looked stunning—his smile ready and easy—reminding her so much of those first few days together they'd had years ago.

So she stared at the horizon, drawing on the beauty

of the water and the balm of the wind. They made good progress and she watched the crew set anchor in a sheltered bay for the night. Tried to maintain her smile for the terribly serious stewards as they presented a five-course silver-service dinner. But being surrounded by effervescent yet nervous young people was perfect. They were ideal chaperones, protecting her from making more mistakes.

She was debating whether it was safer to stay late on deck or risk her cabin and that dangerous closeness to Ares when one young steward appeared.

'We've a surprise for you up on the top deck,' she said.

'Oh, how lovely.' Bethan avoided meeting the amusement in Ares's eyes. 'We'll come up shortly.'

She was slightly nervous about what the surprise could be. Dancers? Musicians?

But when she followed the steward to the deck her heart—and resistance—was torn. They'd set up a cosy nook on the deck with candles, cushions, soft blankets.

'We thought you'd like to star bathe.' The steward beamed.

Star bathe? Bethan nodded—of course, with a barely there waning moon, the sky was awash with millions of stars. They even had a telescope set up.

'There's hot cocoa, a chocolate fondue and you can toast marshmallows,' the steward added.

'This is beautiful, thank you,' Bethan said softly.

It was also unbearably romantic.

'Thanks, team,' Ares added. 'Once you've cleaned up below you can turn in for the night.'

Bethan couldn't resist sinking into the soft cushions,

tilting her head back to appreciate the infinite beauty of the night sky.

'You don't want them to fetch your knitting?' he teased.

She didn't have the focus to knit. She would drop stitches and ruin the pattern. 'I don't want to turn on any lights and ruin the starscape.' She would keep conversation on the crew. It was safe. 'I felt nervous for them but they've done such a great job. If I'd had to serve you at their age, I'd have been so terrified I'd have probably spilled soup in your lap.'

'Am I an ogre?' he asked dryly. 'Or is it just the billionaire status?'

'Neither of those things.' She chuckled sadly. 'You're not scary, they just want to please you. They want your approval—not for the billions, you just have a potency about you.'

'I'm not anyone special, Bethan.'

'Ares—'

He moved jerkily. 'I'm not. I already told you I was the son of no man and worth nothing.' His eyes were barely visible in the low lamplight but still she saw the shadows.

'You forget the Vasiliadis family are very good at keeping their shame hidden,' he said.

'You could never be anyone's shame,' she murmured.

'Oh, but I am, Bethan.' Bitterness bled through every word.

She turned her gaze to the sky above and whispered the question he'd probably never answer. 'How?'

Sure enough there was silence. She guessed he was likely counting. And she regretted asking—he didn't want any intimacy other than the physical with her. And it seemed he didn't even want that now. She stared up at the stars—so beautiful, but cold.

'My mother was a water witch,' he said softly. 'She grew up on a northern island. Was a strong swimmer, loved sailing. She wanted a career on the water—could have been a captain had she been given fair training, fair treatment.'

Bethan bit her lip, stopping herself interrupting, sensing his mother hadn't gotten any of those things.

'She worked locally for a while, then went to Athens, wanting to break into the bigger boat scene. Better tips. Better travel opportunities. She was adventurous. She got a job as a steward, serving the arrogant wealthy jerks you're not so fond of, and one took what he wanted from her.'

'Loukas Vasiliadis,' Bethan muttered after a long silence.

'She was young and he was in a position of power and their affair wasn't an equal relationship on any level,' he said. 'She'd known he was married but believed him when he said it was over. When she told him she was pregnant he didn't want her to have the baby. Turned out his wife was also pregnant. He cut her off. She didn't want to return home and bring that shame on her parents. She went from the boats to bottom-rung cleaning jobs—scraping together as much money as she could to get through. Alex and I were born three months apart. Him into that palatial compound, me into a one-room flat. My mother kept working but it was a hand-to-mouth existence and Loukas Vasiliadis never helped.'

Bethan waited for several beats but couldn't resist asking—hoping he'd answer again. 'But then he died?'

'I was thirteen,' Ares said quietly. 'They were in a small plane. Loukas was teaching Alex to fly but it decompressed and they died from hypoxia long before it crashed. My grandfather Pavlos knew I existed, wanted his bloodline to continue and, as I was the only option, the rest of the family were forced to accept me.'

Her heart pounded. 'So you never actually met Alex.'

'No.'

'And never your father?'

He shook his head.

'So Pavlos just found you and said welcome to the family? What did your mother say?'

Ares stared into the small flame. Burned his marshmallow. Set it to the side—ignoring the small burn on the tips of his fingers as he did. He'd intended to tell her about the foundation but somehow had gotten sidetracked with family history. But the two were intertwined and he couldn't explain the first without revealing something of the second. Just not everything. Not the greatest shame of all.

'My mother lost her future when she had me,' he said huskily. 'Lost her chance of building the career she wanted. On the water, like your father. She couldn't go away for weeks at a time when there was no one else to care for me. So when Pavlos came for me, it gave her a chance to have the life she'd missed out on. The freedom to finally reach for her own goals.'

A worried look flickered across her face. 'And she wanted that then?'

He paused. Some parts he had to skip.

'Pavlos took my education very seriously. In his view I'd not even had the basics and to be worthy of the Vasiliadis name I needed to earn it. Become the complete package. I worked hard to learn, to fit in. Because for a long time my plan was to gain control, ultimately take over completely, then I was going to tear the dynasty down from the inside.'

'You wanted revenge.'

Of course. Because it was only when he'd become 'useful' that they'd bothered to show up. But they'd ripped him away from his home. 'They changed everything. Made me change my name. My mother wasn't mentioned. There was interest, of course, but the narrative was quietly spread that she wasn't able to care for me, so people were too polite to say anything to my face. It wasn't long before she was entirely forgotten.'

Publicly he'd been enfolded into the Vasiliadis family—but hardly held close. And he couldn't really blame them.

'How did Gia treat you?' Bethan asked.

There'd been nothing but resentment and mistrust in the Vasiliadis compound.

'She was soon involved with Dion. They wanted to retain as much control over the operation as possible but I didn't let that happen.'

'Sophia.' Bethan's gaze flicked to his, then away again.

'We kissed once, when we were young. She wanted to marry me as little as I wanted to marry her.' He half smiled, at her flicker of jealousy. 'They planted those stories. Trying to shame me into it. As if public expectation would sway me.'

The extended Vasiliadis family hadn't wanted him but they'd had no choice because blood had mattered. They'd groomed him and up to a point he'd allowed it. But to interfere in his choice of life partner? Never.

None of that had been in his mind the day he'd met Bethan. He'd gone to the island villa to be alone and free for a while. He'd bought the villa in his early twenties, needed the space to decompress. Naïve and earnest, unbearably pretty Bethan had basically barged her way onto his boat. He'd been unable to resist giving her the lift and by the time they'd made it to the island, he'd known he would have her. She'd been the sweetest, sexiest thing. Scandalous, succulent curves made for him. He couldn't get enough—knew he would never get enough. He'd known deprivation and his need for her was a craving that would never be satisfied. So he'd asked her to marry him. Absolute *madness*.

'Maybe marriage was in the back of my mind because of their constant references. And I didn't give you a lot of time to think about it. I just made assumptions based on what little I knew and arranged everything. I shouldn't have. I'm sorry.'

'Fools rush in.' She patted his damned hand as if he were the one who needed soothing. 'I did say yes, you know. I'm equally to blame.'

Ah, no. She'd been a grieving and lonely romantic, swept off her feet by the speed and dreaminess of it all. She'd ached for happiness. Instead he'd hurt her.

'But I *was* your revenge,' she added quietly.

'*Never,*' he breathed. 'You were never that. When Pavlos died I took over as CEO—sooner than anyone expected—but I'd worked so hard to gain more and more control and in doing that I'd realised that a lot of people depend on the companies for their survival. We have so many employees. Taking revenge on my family by destroying the company wouldn't have been right.'

'So you no longer want revenge?'

'I want justice,' he said.

She frowned. 'For your mother?'

He nodded. 'They wouldn't name her. Wouldn't let me name her. Wouldn't acknowledge her.'

They'd destroyed her. But so had Ares. He was equally to blame.

'But when you went to the Vasiliadis compound, did she revive her career?'

He couldn't bear to think of her life after he'd left. 'She was treated so badly. She should have had better options far earlier. I want her foundation to make that difference to those young people.'

'If you were so busy doing all the things they insisted on, she must have missed you.'

'Missed me?' The long-held agony burst forth. 'I *never* wanted to go with them. Never wanted to leave her. But I had no choice because she said she was tired of working three jobs to support me! That I was a burden and she was thrilled because she could finally be free of me!'

In the stunned silence he clawed to recover his breath. His emotional control. But couldn't.

'I was so *angry*,' he growled. 'I wanted to prove to *them* that I could do any impossible thing they set for me and I wanted to punish *her* for making me go with them. So I didn't visit her and she didn't contact me. It was a stand-off. Neither of us gave in.'

He glanced at Bethan. Her expression was pinched, her skin pale despite the gold light from the flickering flame. And his composure cracked again. Because it was how he'd treated her, no? He'd gone silent. Cold. It was what he did. The Vasiliadis in him. The realisation twisted his insides. 'I had all these stupid plans,' he admitted feebly, wanting her to know he wasn't entirely awful. 'I was going to buy her a new home and her own damned boat. I wanted her to be so...'

Proud. And sorry. He closed his eyes. He'd wanted her to want him again.

Even though now as an adult he could rationalise his mother's actions—that perhaps she'd said all that because she'd thought the move was best for him, that he would have opportunities she couldn't give him—it *still* devastated him. Because she'd once given him what no one else had—the belief that he was actually wanted for *himself.* Just Ares. Just a boy. With no money, no power. They'd had a nice life together, no? It hadn't been entirely a burden. But she'd destroyed that belief and he'd been unable to rebuild it. Not completely.

'She didn't revive her career. It was too late and she didn't have any money to get ahead. They didn't even pay her off. And because I wouldn't contact her, I never knew she injured her back on a job and went on painkillers to keep working. Never knew she got addicted.' He winced at Bethan's small sound of distress. 'I didn't know she'd died until three days later.'

His mother had never reached out to tell him she'd been hurt. She'd tried to deal with it on her own—masking her pain and keeping working those crappy jobs. She'd not given him a *chance* to help her. He was so hurt by that even though it was what he'd deserved for never going back to check on her. And all his effort to become the most powerful Vasiliadis heir had been for *nothing*.

'Ares, I'm so sorry.'

'It doesn't matter.'

Bethan didn't call him out on the pathetic lie. Nor did she ask any more questions. She just kept her hand on his, leaned her shoulder lightly against his, a calm counterpoint to the turmoil of emotions he couldn't handle.

He watched the little flame burn lower as the gas depleted, too spent to regret telling her about that horrifying day. He'd never before told anyone what his mother had done. What he'd done in childish retaliation. The consequences unable to be rectified.

There was nothing to be said to make it better—it simply was—and he appreciated that Bethan didn't try. He didn't move—couldn't—when she was a heavier weight now and anchoring him in place. But he still couldn't sleep. He couldn't shut his damned brain down. He couldn't ever get peace.

CHAPTER NINE

BETHAN BLINKED AT the bright blue sky, slowly realising she was ensconced in a nest of soft blankets. Alone. Scraps of conversation flayed her heart.

I didn't visit her...she didn't contact me...

He'd been so hurt. So *alone*. For years.

Maybe marriage was in the back of my mind... I didn't give you a lot of time...

She got to the cabin without seeing anyone. She swiftly showered and changed but despite pulling herself together physically, she could still barely cope with the internal impact of that quietly emotional conversation. Of course she appreciated his honesty and trust in telling her all he had, but it changed everything. Before it had been easy to consider him a heartless, callous villain who'd used her. Now she couldn't—he was far more human. And yes, hurt. Now she understood more why he'd acted the way he had and she could hardly blame him for keeping his most painful, personal secrets from her when she'd done exactly the same to him.

But it was also clear they *were* over. He'd made no move last night and surely he knew she would have easily acquiesced. But no. They were past lovers simply clearing the air. Except desire festered deep inside her—building again to that dangerous point where there'd be another explosion. For her own well-being she had to contain it. This situation didn't need more complication.

On her way back up she heard voices from the main deck and stopped on the stairs, hoping they'd move on so they wouldn't see her.

'You should ask Bethan to show you.' Ares's voice carried. 'She knows all the knots. I've never seen anyone tie off as fast. Ask if she'll demonstrate and film her. Then practise. Lots. That's what she does.'

'Does she work on boats?'

'No, her father was in the navy and she learned from him,' Ares answered. 'She weaves masterpieces out of all kinds of things. She makes incredibly intricate props for escape rooms.'

'That's so cool.'

'Yeah.'

Bethan blushed hard and her legs lost all strength so she had to lean against the wall. He was bragging about her to the trainee crew. His audible approval—pride—added to her conflicting feelings. Her regret. When she'd cooled enough to keep climbing the stairs she found him on deck demonstrating something with the anchor to four junior deckhands. Apparently he was completely at ease and not at all embarrassed that they'd spent all night up in that nook the stewards had created. Or at least Bethan had—she'd no idea what time Ares had left her. But she remembered the sensation of being held close while sleeping and he must have stopped them from disturbing her given it was well after dawn now.

At least she'd been fully dressed up there. Though that fact also hurt her weak little heart.

'We've been waiting for you.' Ares broke away from the group as soon as he saw her.

'Oh?' She brushed her hair behind her ear and failed to settle her scurrying pulse. 'What did you need me for?'

'Firstly, breakfast.' He turned to the deckhands. 'You guys get those boats ready, okay?'

'Boats?' Bethan followed him to the laden table on the sun deck. Then paused when she was able to look at him properly. 'Are you okay?'

He had shadows beneath his eyes and his clean shave had left him looking slightly pale. 'Just hungry.' He reached for the silver serving tongs to attack the pancake tower.

Pensive, Bethan loaded up on the fresh fruit. The fluffy pancakes were delightful, but she noticed Ares didn't actually eat that much.

'So, boats?' she eventually prompted.

He leaned back in his chair, cradling the mug of tea in his hands. 'We're splitting the trainees into two and racing. The crew have set out a course with a couple of markers.'

'Racing?' A little adrenalin rippled through her. 'You and I against each other?'

'Two crew each.' He smirked. 'Knew that would pique your interest.'

'What's my prize when I win?' she muttered, avoiding his eyes by reaching for more blueberries.

'What do you want it to be?'

She drew a careful breath, failing again to settle her rising pulse. 'I'm sure I'll think of something.'

Half an hour later she let him fasten her life jacket for her. She couldn't resist having him close. Then she looked at the two gleaming boats the crew had sourced from the nearby island.

Last time she and Ares had sailed together in a small sailboat, they'd done it as a team, working in sync to catch the wind. This time they were competitors and equally determined to beat each other. She kept one eye on him, one on the water, felt the breeze and made the calls to her crew. While Ares had local knowledge, Bethan was her father's daughter. She'd spent hours sailing when he was home and was comfortable for the hours they spent beneath the sun now. Ares—inexplicably—was slightly off the pace from the start and stayed that way. Bethan chuckled as her two crew whooped as they crossed the last marker first.

'You're good,' Ares called as they sailed back to the big yacht.

'I had a good crew.' She grinned, feeling the flush of winner's pride.

'It wasn't only the crew,' he drawled as they climbed back on the main deck.

She pressed a hand to her chest in outrage. 'Don't even try to suggest you let me win.'

'Oh, I didn't,' he muttered, leaning against the railing. 'I desperately wanted to beat you and I'm devastated to have failed.'

'Too bad about your call on that last leg.' She unfastened her jacket.

'Yeah.' He huffed out a heavy breath.

Bethan glanced across the water as the trainees sailed the small boats back to the harbour—clearly racing again. She grinned and ran a hand through her sea-sprayed hair.

'You okay, sir?'

She turned, struck by both question and tone. A young second officer stood on the other side of Ares who had, in fact, lost more colour.

'Are you sure I can't get you something?'

Ares stiffened—barriers sliding back into place—and murmured something short in Greek. The officer immediately looked awkward.

'He's pale because losing isn't something he's used to,' Bethan joked lightly, but stepped between Ares and the officer. 'I appreciate your thoroughness,' she said quietly. 'I'll call if we need you.'

The youth bowed and couldn't get off the deck fast enough. Bethan turned back to Ares.

'I'm fine,' he said but he took a seat.

'You're not. You're *good* with those kids, for you to snap at him…' She trailed off and frowned.

Ares was clearly counting again. Slow, steady counting to facilitate deep, even breaths. He'd obviously been taught to. Why? Suddenly queasy, she moved closer.

'I know,' he finally sighed. 'I shouldn't have. I didn't want…' He caught her eye. 'This is nothing.'

She hunched in front of him so he couldn't hide his face from her. He'd not wanted that attention. Too bad. 'Obviously it's not nothing. What's going on? In sickness and health, remember, husband?'

He shot her a smile but it barely held his usual cynicism. 'You left. You broke those vows already.'

'What's going on?' She ignored him. 'Tell me.'

Bending closer, he cupped her face, then fluttered his fingers down the column of her neck. 'Make me.'

'Don't try to distract me—'

'I'm not trying to distract you,' he growled. 'I just can't keep my hands off you any longer.'

'No.' Despite the leap in *her* pulse, she grabbed his wrists and held his hands still at her throat. '*Talk* to me, Ares. I'm worried.'

His eyes widened as he looked into hers and he sighed. 'I'm sorry. It really is nothing,' he reassured too gently. 'You don't need to worry.'

'Then what's the problem with telling me?' Her anxiety wasn't soothed in the slightest.

'Since when were you so stubborn?' Tenderness softened his smirk.

Since she'd found her confidence—her *fight*. She eyeballed him. She was stubborn *now*. This time she wasn't letting him deflect or distract. She was not walking away without knowing everything. This was too important. Was something really wrong? 'Why are you so scared of talking to me?' Her voice rose. She'd cared for her grandmother for years. She didn't want him to be unwell. 'What do you think I can possibly do to you?'

He stared down into her face, his gaze roving over her features, his mouth twisted in remorse. 'It was an anxiety attack,' he said quietly.

'*What?*'

'You're not the only one who feels stressed sometimes. You babble, my heart goes too fast.' He shrugged.

Anxiety?

'Don't make more out of it,' Ares said.

'It's happened before?' Her brain raced and *her* panic rose.

'I'd been working long hours and one afternoon I found myself on the floor.'

'You *collapsed*?' Cold fear flooded her. That sounded like a lot more than anxiety. Her heart battered her ribs, making her breathless. 'Did you see someone about it?'

'Yes. The doctors did far more tests than necessary.' His finger stroked slowly, soothing as she gripped his wrists more tightly. 'It wasn't my heart. There's no damage or anything. I'd just done too many hours on not enough sleep and needed a bit of a break.'

But he was *still* struggling with it.

'Did you tell anyone?' she asked.

His face was six inches from hers. Fiercely she gazed into his eyes, needing to know he was telling her the truth.

'Let them know I had a weak moment? Never. I went to the villa for some time out and reassessed my priorities.' He smiled at her. 'I really am fine, Bethan. You don't need to worry. I promise.'

So he'd created this new foundation for his mother and, Bethan realised, decided to finalise their divorce. Clearly he wanted closure on personal things. Stressful things. Like her too.

'Did you sleep at all last night?' she whispered.

His gaze dropped. No, he hadn't. She suspected he hadn't slept much the night before either.

She held two fingers on the inside of his wrist. 'Your pulse *is* fast.'

'That's not from panic.' Colour returned to his cheeks. 'I really am okay. I don't need any medication. The doctors said I'm fine. I work on relaxation, eating well, not doing as many long hours.'

He *worked* on them. The carefree Ares she'd met, *holiday* Ares, was a rare creature. She wanted to bring him back here now. She knew how—the way that had always been so easy for them.

'Relaxation, you say?' Bethan made a show of pondering. 'You need to rest now. Maybe you'd better lie down for a bit.'

His eyes kindled. 'Maybe that's not a bad idea.'

She lifted his hands from her neck as she stood but kept hold of his wrist. He rose and she led him to her cabin. He said nothing as she tugged the hem of his tee, just lifted his arms so she could strip him out of it. His swim shorts followed so he was naked in mere moments. She pushed and he sank onto the bed. He patted the space beside him, colour fully restored. He *was* fit, but he was *tired*. That was still evident. While she was feeling wired—not from the win, but the sudden worry and the ensuing spike of adrenalin and relief at his insistence that all this wasn't anything serious. *Yet.* Which meant it was still possibly serious. But right now she was relieved he was okay, relieved he still wanted her and she would help him *relax*.

'You're leaving?' He frowned as she walked away. 'You think I'm not up for sex?'

She turned back and raked her gaze down his body again. Oh, he was definitely up.

'Wouldn't want you to have a heart attack from overexerting yourself,' she teased.

'You could take charge.'

'Oh, Ares, didn't you realise?' She smiled at him as she wriggled out of her damp clothes. 'I'm already in charge.'

She dug about in her craft bag then held out her hand. He let her take his wrist again. But when she raised it above his head, he stiffened.

'What are you doing?' he muttered.

'Utilising the knots you told those kids I'm good at.' She wound wool around his wrist—loosely enough but still secure.

'You heard me?'

'I did.' She smiled. 'You're good with them. And I *am* good at knots.'

It wouldn't take a huge effort for him to rip free from them but he didn't. He even let her bind his other wrist above his head.

'This is more than taking charge,' he pointed out.

She watched the restless roll of his hips and felt her excitement rise. 'I'm going to make you relax, Ares. But we both know it'll only be as far as you let me.'

Another ripple of tension swept down him. 'What is it you're planning to do?'

'Everything.' She found condoms in the bedside table, fully appreciating how perfectly stocked the yacht was. 'But you have to let me know if I take things too far.' She ran her fingertip down his stomach.

'Mmmm.' He sucked in his cheeks.

She crawled onto the bed, prowling up to kneel astride him. 'I'm going to keep a close eye on your pulse.'

He watched her hands slide towards his centre. 'My *pulse*, huh?'

'Well, this is where all your blood seems to have gone.'

He laughed weakly. 'Bethan…'

'You just relax and I'll do my thing.' She brushed her lips over the tip of his erection in the lightest tease. 'Then you might get some sleep.'

'You do…uh…*that*.' His breath whistled as she kissed him.

He had the most fantastic body. Some of it might be good genes, but she suspected he didn't just work long hours, he put decent sessions in the gym too. When *did* he rest these days? She would make him—she would wear him out entirely. But he was right, so often there were many reasons behind life choices—including selfish ones. And this certainly wasn't all benevolence on her behalf. She was desperately hungry—so tempted by his large, hard erection. Desire commanded her. He muttered her name, over and over until he couldn't form the word any more. His breathing deepened—then was broken by sighs. She moved faster as he rocked his hips but she knew he was resisting release.

'You know I'm so into this,' he suddenly gasped. 'But I do think it could be better.'

Outraged, she glanced up and tightened her grip on the base of his cock. '*Excuse* me?'

Devilry danced in his eyes. 'I want you to turn around,' he whispered breathlessly. 'And bring that hot wet piece of you up here where I can taste it.'

He backed up the invitation with a jerk of his hips, bumping her from where she sat on his strong thighs.

'We're both winners then, right?' he added.

Her mouth on him. His mouth on her. Oh, but he was a tease—and irresistible. Even when bound he took control and she was thrilled to let him. But she teased back, taking her time to crawl up his body and sit as he'd suggested. She closed her eyes when he touched her with his tongue—teasing her to the point where she could hardly concentrate on what she was doing. Both moaned—a sensual symphony. His urgency increased—he loved pleasuring her. She grabbed his shaft, opened her lips and took him deeper than ever. Heard his animal grunts as his hot release spurted into her mouth and her own orgasm hit.

'Sleepy now?' she queried, sliding to sit beside him.

'No.' But he was trembling.

She placed her hand on his chest, felt the strong beat of his heart. 'You should rest.'

'You shouldn't deny me,' he countered. 'I can't take the strain.'

She gazed, revelling in his bulging body again. 'Ares...'

'Please.'

He was such a challenge. But one she was delighted to rise to.

Quivering with renewed excitement, she struggled to work the condom down his thick, hard cock. 'Sorry,' she mumbled with a laugh.

'Don't apologise again. Ever,' he growled. 'This is the best view of my life. Just don't stop.'

She smiled. 'Are you begging?'

'God, yes.'

Circling her hips, she took only the tip of him inside her, teasing him briefly before plunging down. His groan hit her soul. She lifted and sank on him again, her head dropping back at the sheer pleasure of having him like this. All *hers*. His gaze was locked on her—hot and fierce and he thrust to meet her faster, harder.

She braced—her hands wide on his bunched biceps—taking the reins again and riding him as ferociously as she could—driving him to the point where he couldn't control anything any more. Not her. And most definitely not himself. She watched as ecstasy overtook him—destroyed him. And her own joy hit.

'You're killing me, Bethan,' he muttered.

'Can't have that.' She reached up and tugged on the yarn. The knots released instantly and he wrapped her in a bear hug, dragging her down to snuggle against him.

'Pleased with yourself?' he drawled.

'And with you, yes.' She tapped her fingers across his chest and burrowed closer.

'Mmmm.'

To her delight he sounded drowsy. She closed her eyes and her contentment deepened when she felt his limbs go heavier. He was asleep. Seconds later, so was she. But it felt like only moments before he spoke again.

'Bethan, you need to get up.'

It took effort to open her eyes. The moment she did, she sat up. Ares was dressed. In a *suit*.

'What time is it?' Amazed, she glanced at the porthole and glimpsed a chink of light. 'Is it *morning*?' Had they slept not just through the afternoon, but the entire night?

'Yes.' The regret in his eyes was unsettling enough, but his next words horrified her. 'We're in Athens.'

CHAPTER TEN

Ares watched Bethan quietly knot, release, then re-knot a rubber band. Tried not to think about how those nimble fingers had wrecked him yesterday. The deepest sleep he'd had in years had followed. He should be happy about that, no? That it had been all light play and laughter—the easiest burn of their lingering chemistry. But now his stomach was knotting and unknotting itself as regret spiralled around him. He wished they'd not yet arrived in Athens. But his assistant Theo waited on the dock and drove them to the apartment. Bethan went into the room she'd used the night he'd brought her here. He set his bag down and stared out of the window. Then went to her door.

'I need to go to the office to check the final arrangements. Do you have something to wear tonight?'

'I can figure something out,' Bethan said.

'Take Theo. He'll translate and pay for anything you need.'

'Thanks.' She smiled peaceably. 'I'd like to present well for you tonight.'

The knots in his stomach doubled when she didn't put up any resistance to his offer. Was she treating him with kid gloves? He shouldn't have told her about the attack. Though she'd hardly taken it easy on him yesterday afternoon. It hadn't been pity sex, but all passion. Maybe they could have more.

He went to work while he still had the strength. He ran through the notes for his speech, messages, checked the decorations and other preparations. Then went to his barber. Halfway through the trim, his phone chimed. He looked at the message and felt the familiar disappointment kick. This family would *always* reject him personally so this was no real surprise yet still stupidly painful.

He drove back to the apartment. Bethan wasn't there but he wasn't worried—she'd taken Theo, who'd sent an update. He showered, dressed, went out to the lounge, avoiding the crystal decanters, and brewed a thick coffee instead. Damn the doctors, he needed the hit.

'Do I look okay?'

He turned and forgot the coffee. Didn't need it because energy flooded every cell. Bethan was in the doorway wearing a white, sexy, demure, delight of a dress. One strap barely rested on her right shoulder, looking as if it was about to slip. It was cut low across her fantastic breasts and hugged her waist before flaring into a full skirt that ended at her knees, displaying the full abundance of her hourglass, heavenly figure. His mouth gummed. Desire took command of his brain—teasing him with a billion ideas of what to do with her in that dress, right *now*. His beautiful wife—about to be *ex*-wife—was exquisite. How anyone was going to concentrate on anything anyone said or did, he didn't know. He certainly wasn't going to be able to.

'Ares?'

'I…' He reached for a polite, appropriate response but the words wouldn't come because he was stripped raw. Weakened by it. Honesty rose, entwined with total regret, and he sank back against the countertop. 'You don't have to come tonight if you don't want to.'

Her eyes widened, pained.

'You look beautiful,' he rushed to add, realising his mistake. 'It's just that I shouldn't have made you do this.'

She breathed. Moved closer. 'You've not made me do anything I haven't wanted to this whole week, Ares.' Soft, proud, stunning.

He bowed his head, avoiding her too-forgiving eyes. 'I realise I never finished explaining about the foundation,' he muttered. 'I don't want my life to have been about making more money for a family I don't even like. I need something more. So Melina's name is there and her story—in part—is told because I want other young people empowered and taken care of. They should have a safe working environment and a decent support network.' He glanced up. 'I'm deliberately holding it at Vasiliadis headquarters. I've put a huge amount of company money in, much to the family's discomfort. My mother's experience wasn't unique unfortunately. But for her to be erased—that's not right. I won't let it happen any more. This night is for her.'

'Good for you,' she murmured.

He gazed at the empathy shimmering in her eyes. At her dignity. He reached into his pocket and pulled out his phone. Showed her the message. 'Apparently the family are all unwell with a viral infection. Flu or some such. Naturally they don't want to pass it on to my guests so none of them are able to make it.' Not Gia or Dion, nor his aunt or any of the 'cousins' who enjoyed the compound. 'Gia is sure I understand.'

It was a lie of course. Security told him Gia had been in and out of the offices all week and not been coughing or sneezing at all.

'Ares—'

'It doesn't matter.' He didn't want pity. Didn't want to dwell on the fact that they would never accept or acknowledge his lineage. That they would never support something he cared about. They were interested only in him building the business into a bigger enterprise that just made them even more money.

'Well, for what it's worth...' Bethan cupped the side of his face '... *I'll* be there.'

Just like that she was the nearest thing to an ally he'd ever had. He caught her hand in his and felt the press of something hard against his palm. He bent to study her fingers. She curled them but he didn't let her tug away.

'I thought I should wear my wedding ring, seeing we're acting as if...as if...'

Not just the wedding band, but the extravagant engagement ring he'd ordered in such a rush. He stared at the platinum-set gleaming diamond he'd given her. He didn't know why he'd chosen that one. He'd relied on the jeweller, gone traditional. He wouldn't now. She needed something with more colour and flare. Perhaps a ruby to match her mouth, set in gold to rest against the warmth of her skin and heart. But tonight the ice-like diamond was a stunning match not just for the dress but for her luminosity. She simply shone.

'I can take them off,' she muttered.

He tightened his grip. She'd brought them with her—

probably to give them back. She wouldn't want to keep them but they should be worn once more. 'Leave it. It's perfect. Thank you for thinking of it.'

Her lashes dropped, hiding her deep gaze, but he couldn't stop staring as if hoping to read everything within her. Every person in the room was going to stare at her. And want her. Most especially him.

He'd never been more glad of his driver to get them both safely there, given his concentration was so shot, but his problems only deepened once they got there. The place was already packed. Everyone had turned up to this most unusual of Vasiliadis parties. One where no other members of his family appeared. Everyone else was curious as hell about his mother.

Bethan didn't anchor him, she was his North Star. She swept through the room looking an absolute goddess—bright and sparkling—drawing everyone's attention and charming them. Charming *him*.

Several of the trainee crew from *Artemis* were there. He watched her animatedly chatter with them. Yes, she was not shy now—for a guileless artistic, sensitive soul, she could schmooze surprisingly well. The awkward young woman he'd met on the jetty almost two and a half years ago now shimmered. She'd clearly been living her best life in London for her confidence to blossom like this.

'You're magnificent,' he murmured, unable to keep his distance. 'My poor projects manager doesn't know where to look. Everyone is trying really hard not to stare at you.'

'Because they probably think I'm a ghost,' she quipped. 'Your missing wife.'

He chuckled. 'You know you're captivating them.'

'I'm channelling my inner Elodie.' She grinned up at him. 'Wait 'til you meet her, you'll see what I mean.'

He didn't respond. A breath later she bit her lip and glanced away. Because of course he wouldn't meet Elodie or the friend she was knitting all the baby clothing for. She would return to London, divorced, and resume her life. Her best life.

He stepped away again. Unsettled despite the clear success of the evening. All the billionaires present—and there were several—had dug deep to bolster the foundation's account. All supporting the goal of ensuring a safe working environment—free from sexual harassment—for the yachting staff. He glanced at the photo of his mother—displayed in the centre of the photo array. It had been taken before she'd met Loukas Vasiliadis. Before she'd given birth to him. She was on the water, standing in a small boat, her smile wide. She looked happy and young with the world ahead of her. He'd found it crumpled in a box thrown together by uninterested, careless workers. There'd been only two boxes of personal papers. The rest of her effects—her clothing, books, crockery—had been either donated or destroyed. Ares hadn't even been given the chance to return to their small apartment, to go through it himself and revisit those memories. There *had* been good ones there. But he would not hide the circumstances of his birth any more.

Illegitimacy wasn't his source of shame. That was born from his own treatment of his mother. He'd not been a good son. Not checked on her. Not helped her. He'd been hurt and angry.

He'd thought if he did this, if he ensured she was honoured, not forgotten, it might assuage some of that guilt, but now he had it didn't give any true satisfaction. He still felt bad. It wasn't enough and never would be. His mother would never see this. Futility swamped him. He was a failure.

Bethan circulated on the periphery, taking a breather by studying the pictures on display to demonstrate the foundation's projects that were already in action. Naturally the party was an outstanding success—there was quite the joyous vibe. The young people present were excited and enjoying it as they should. Their infectious energy made her smile. She paused, surprised by one photo. It was of Ares and *her* taken while they were racing only yesterday on the two little yachts. The shot had them both in frame—he was laughing, his pallor masked by that wide smile. She was in front, both crew working hard. She didn't blame him for showing it. It was to sell the success of the foundation and perhaps to show personal unity—all part of his plan to make this a success, and good for him for wanting to do something more than make money. Her heart ached. She'd had no idea he was so alone.

She glanced across the room to find him watching her. He extricated himself but immediately was intercepted by another man. His facade slid in place. Working hard.

'You must be pleased with the evening.'

Bethan turned at the quiet voice and stiffened. Sophia Dimou stood beside her. Surprise silenced her—Ares had said none of the Vasiliadis extended family were coming. But *Sophia* had shown up for him and she looked particularly stunning. Certainly the tall man by her side seemed to think so, given he couldn't take his gaze off her.

'Bethan, this is my fiancé, Felipe. Felipe, this is Ares's wife, Bethan.' Sophia smiled.

'Pleased to meet you, Bethan.' Felipe smiled, full-wattage charm.

The man's presence didn't soothe the jealousy that flared within Bethan. Because this time she wasn't jealous that Ares had once kissed Sophia, but of the happiness evident between Sophia and her Felipe.

'It's lovely to see you here,' Sophia added quietly.

'You too.' Bethan tried hard to smile.

'I hope we'll get to see a lot more of you.' Sophia leaned closer. 'I remember Ares was so happy when he first told me about you.'

Bethan weakly gave in to curiosity. 'Oh?'

'He gave me advance warning because the family were pressuring us into marrying and he didn't want me to suffer any fallout. I did get a bit but it's worked out okay. He and I knew our getting together was ridiculous. *Never* going to happen.' She moved closer, her voice dropping. 'Honestly, I used to be scared of him. He was so cold when he moved into the compound but I guess he was lonely.' She smiled again. 'I'm really glad you're back with him.'

Bethan could only nod, relieved when Sophia moved to talk to someone else, Felipe a tall presence beside her.

Of *course* Ares had been cold when he'd moved into that compound. He'd just been abandoned by his mother and dragged into the home of the dead father who'd refused to acknowledge him. There he'd faced the woman who'd just lost her husband and son. His grandfather had been beyond cruel with his insane expectations.

Bethan was mad that she'd been such a fool back then, too dazzled and dreamy to ask proper questions. She'd assumed all would miraculously work out instead of speaking up and finding out. Now she glanced around and caught Ares's gaze. He clearly wasn't paying much attention to the men yapping next to him, given he was already staring at her. She registered the space about him—an aura, like an invisible shell setting him apart. Defence. Isolation. Because tonight was deeply personal. Deeply painful. Despite all he'd done, he was still unhappy.

She moved towards him, her emotion kindled. He broke away from the group and met her halfway.

Bethan read restlessness in his expression. 'Are you not pleased with how it's going?' She pressed her hand on his arm and his muscles tensed beneath her fingers. 'It's an amazing night. The foundation is an amazing achievement. You should be so proud. Honestly, Ares, it's all amazing. You're so generous.' *He* was amazing.

She stiffened, embarrassed that she wasn't just back to babbling awkwardly, she was gushing—inanely repeating herself. 'Not that you need me to tell you that.'

His gaze was very intense. 'No, I appreciate your support.'

She lost a few seconds in his eyes and suddenly had to turn away before she said other stupid things that he wouldn't want to hear from her. Things she couldn't take back. 'I'm just going to freshen up before you give your speech,' she murmured. 'Back soon.'

Flustered, she walked out of the ballroom and off in the wrong direction. She wandered half the floor on a quest to find another restroom. She rounded a corner, about to give up, when a door ahead opened.

Bethan froze, instantly recognising the older woman in the sleek designer suit. Gia Vasiliadis. So she was here in the building but not showing up for Ares.

Gia clearly recognised her too—if her pinched expression was anything to go by.

Bethan assumed calm as the woman approached. 'You've been here all night but not bothered to show—'

'As if you've shown up at any time in the last two or so years,' Gia interrupted acerbically.

She snuck a breath. 'As if that isn't what you wanted.' Hit by Gia's bitterness, she stepped back and tried to remember the bigger picture, because this was so very complicated. 'I know I wasn't the woman you wanted in his life.' She worked to soften her tone. 'I know he wasn't the son you wanted to take over all this.'

She felt sorry for the woman but surely enough time had passed for Gia to see beyond her own pain and that others had suffered too.

'Ares's father's behaviour was not his fault. Nor his *grandfather's* behaviour,' Bethan pointed out huskily. 'Pavlos bringing Ares to your home in the midst of your grief must have been terribly difficult.'

Gia stood like an ice sculpture, but her eyes widened.

Bethan had blamed—at times *hated*—Gia for the doubts she'd seeded in Bethan's head. But it had been Bethan's mistake to be so reactive. Now older—having lived that bit more—she saw more. Understood more. Perhaps even had the smallest insight into the immensity of Gia's heartbreak. She too knew loss. This woman had lost her husband *and* her only child and then her husband's other son had been brought into her home. They'd *all* suffered for this family—because for Pavlos Vasiliadis the preservation of the dynasty was more important than anything personal. All that had mattered was blood lineage.

Gia had bought into that too, with her desire to unite her line with Ares through Sophia. Cousins and cousins—all to claim power and control. There'd never been a loving welcome but there was always more to a situation than what appeared, facets to the people involved. Nothing was ever as simple as villains and heroes. Now Bethan saw beyond her fairy-tale blinkers, saw something of the vulnerability they *all* shared. And she had her voice.

'Since Ares arrived, he's done almost everything you asked of him. That the Vasiliadis dynasty asked of him,' she said. 'Yet still he gets no support for something that's deeply personal and important to him?'

'Would you stomach having your husband's lover honoured in front of you?' Gia spat. 'You would accept that humiliation?'

'Your husband's behaviour wasn't *your* fault either,' Bethan said bluntly. 'And she was *barely* your husband's lover. But she will always be Ares's mother. She deserves her place in his life. This is not all about *you*.'

'What do you care?' Gia glared at her. 'Why now?'

Bethan swallowed and sidestepped the question. 'Ares has my full support. Because what Ares does is good.' She stared at the woman. 'You should appreciate all he's done for the family you all proclaim is so important. You should—'

'Ares,' Gia interrupted her, her gaze lifting.

Bethan turned, heart seizing. Ares stood only a few feet away and he was looking right into her eyes. She couldn't look away from him. Prickly heat suffused her skin. She'd overstepped.

'I will be able to make a brief appearance after all,' Gia said. 'Unfortunately Dion is still indisposed at the compound.'

Stiffly Gia stalked past, heading towards the ballroom. But Ares didn't follow her. He remained staring at Bethan.

'How much did you hear?' she asked guiltily, moving closer to him.

'All of it.' He cleared his throat.

Oh. 'I'm sorry.' She faced him, braced for his displeasure. 'I know I didn't need to defend you and I didn't really cause a scene. I don't think anyone else saw.'

He lifted his hand and brushed her lips with the backs of his fingers. 'I thought you weren't going to apologise for having a sweet nature any more.'

'I'm not sure I was all that sweet just then.'

The corner of his mouth lifted. 'You were...'

She leaned closer, but he didn't finish the sentence. He just gazed at her mouth a moment too long. She didn't care about what he'd been going to say, she wanted him to kiss her. But he stepped back.

'I'd better go back and minimise whatever damage Gia's about to do,' he sighed.

'And you still have to do your speech.'

'Right.' He reached out and took her hand.

It was for show, right? That unity to project. They went back to the convivial vibes. From her place beside Ares she watched Gia. The older woman was a walking polite smile, rocking a facade as bullet-proof as Ares so often did. She took in the pictures, sipped from a champagne flute, lasted a full forty minutes—even through all Ares's speech. Which she applauded. And when she then approached Ares, the crowds stepped back.

'Congratulations, Ares,' she said. 'This is impressive. It will be good for our future yachting employees.'

'Thank you, Gia.' Ares matched her formality. 'I appreciate your effort to be here when I know you aren't feeling a hundred per cent.'

A moment later, Bethan watched Gia depart, honestly stunned. She didn't kid herself that everything was suddenly fine. As if a few words from her could heal more than a decade of hurt and loss. Gia had been stilted and perhaps it had only been for public show but Bethan hoped there'd been even a vestige of genuine acceptance. But Ares still had that facade. A few words couldn't breach wounds like his. She breathed again, trying to ease her tension but her heart felt bound by too-tight ropes and it ached to burst free and bloom big. It just ached. Because she couldn't say any of this to him.

'Come on,' Ares said shortly, taking her hand in his again. 'I've had enough.'

She was silent on the short drive back to the apartment. She refused to babble pointlessly—this night was too momentous for waffle now. Besides which she couldn't get her strained brain to think of anything to say. It was focused on only one thing. His party was over and tomorrow she would see the notary. She would leave

Greece. She would leave him. Which meant tonight was their last night together.

Ares didn't turn on the lights when they stepped inside but there was enough light from the street outside to make patterns on the ceiling and upper walls. Which meant she could see him—just enough. He took her hand and led her to his big bedroom. He said nothing and she couldn't. Her throat hurt—too tight, too tense. It was not saying anything that had gotten her into trouble last time. When she'd run away instead of staying and talking to him. She'd not fought for her fragile marriage. Not given either of them a chance to fix it. And it was too late now, wasn't it? Because everything was different. And Bethan was just that bit scared.

Only then he smiled at her. Then he stepped close. Then slowly—so slowly—Ares slid the zip at the side of her dress down and with a sole, gentle finger nudged the strap from her shoulder. The white fabric slipped to the floor in an easy, slippery rush.

His jaw dropped.

Her strapless bra was pure lace as was the tiny triangle that was her panties—with the little ribbon to hold them up. She'd chosen them deliberately earlier today, spent her last few cents on a provocative outfit—to feel sexy, to force a reaction. And yes, the hunger on his face empowered her. But he didn't quicken—didn't haul her close as she'd expect. No, he moved even more slowly. He stepped back, removed his tie, unfastened his shirt buttons. With careful deliberation he gifted her an erotic display. She drank in the dip and ridges of his muscles that the flicker of shadow and light captured. He was so beautiful she melted inside. But she remained still, not wanting to rush this moment in any way.

Reality hung, heavy and unspoken. This *once* more. Their last night. Their last time to have and hold.

He stepped out of his trousers but left his briefs. He walked closer, his hands fisted at his sides. Until he reached her. And then those fists unfurled. His touch was unbearably gentle. Reverently he traced every inch of her body with the tip of his finger—barely skimming her skin in a dance designed to ignite her senses. The featherlight tease deepened as he pressed a touch harder, then palmed parts of her—her breasts, her thighs. Scorching heat fired within, her entire being was weakening—narrowing to this. Only this. Her need for him. She couldn't stand it. She simply couldn't stand it. And he read her mind, lifting her, placing her how he wanted. She was so willing.

He knelt above her, peeled away the scraps of lace, exposing her to his gaze, to the graze of his teeth and tongue. By the time he stroked between her legs she was already beyond the edge. She was almost broken. He repeated the caress, deepened it. She gasped as he breached her. Moaned louder as he flicked, massaging where she was so very needy. Just as she was about to burst, he drew his finger out. She panted as with a provocative smile he circled her unbearably sensitive spot with the smallest, most relentless of motions designed to drive her even more wild. She arched, moaning louder and faster until he finally gave her his fingers again. She instinctively squeezed hard—the orgasm hit instantly. He growled, pumping faster—twisting his fingers to stroke inside her in a way that made those delicious ripples of pleasure go on and on as she shuddered and quaked and finally *crumbled*.

She panted, spent and yet not. She wanted more but she was so far gone couldn't even beg—she was simply a moaning mess of want and need. He kissed her too gently. Too slowly. Soothing her from that heightened sensitivity before starting the sublime torment all over again.

Ares ached to rip off his briefs, plunge back into her bare and bury his seed deep. Nothing between them. Appalled at his own thinking, he slid down her curves to lave his tongue over her soft, sweet sex and taste her honey all over again. Needing as much intimacy as he could get. Needing to touch every part of her—to imprint himself on her being. He shook with the effort to hold back and rolled on the condom while he still had some semblance of control.

Then he moved. She was with him—her hands seeking to hold, her hips undulating in utter invitation for his possession. But she had her eyes closed. Shutting him out of her soul. He couldn't stand for that. Not tonight. He needed her to look right at him. To *see* him. Feel him. And never deny him.

'Look at me. It's me with you.' He finally broke the wordless spell they'd been in from the moment they'd left the gala. 'It's *me* with you, Bethan.'

Her eyes shot open. Her pupils blown. Her mouth pouting. He'd never seen her look so beautiful.

'Of course it is,' she whispered, her bottomless eyes boring into him. 'It's only ever been you,' she said brokenly.

He stilled. She held his face between her hands. He

felt her move beneath him—lifting her legs and locking them around his hips. He was a millimetre away from being inside her. But he couldn't move.

'I've only ever had you.'

With a guttural groan he lost all control. Her body squeezed on his in delight at his possession, her silken heat sucking him in greedily. *Too soon.* He stilled—driven as deep inside her as he could get. 'Bethan?'

He couldn't breathe. He didn't think he could stand to know—but he couldn't stop himself asking. He gazed right into her beautiful brown eyes. 'No one else in this time?'

Her eyes filled, drowning them both. She breathed hard.

'I made promises too…' Her words hardly sounded. 'I wasn't going to break them. Not until…'

He drew back, rolled his hips and pushed forward again, pleasure arcing to the base of his spine even as his heart tore. 'Until it was over?'

Her eyes filled with tears. 'How could I…?'

He shook his head. 'It wasn't that,' he said harshly. 'It wasn't just that.'

She stared up at him but he was deep inside her—not only with his body. He would know her truth. He wouldn't let her hide anything from him.

'You didn't *want* anyone else.' He thrust into her again with a deliberately fierce impact. Daring her to deny him.

But she didn't. She just melted. He felt the rippling wave of acceptance—her body enveloped him in a sensual heat that scorched from the tips of his ears to the soles of his feet. But his heart—his heart was eviscerated.

'I never wanted anyone else,' she whispered. 'Not before. Not since.'

Not ever.

She didn't say those last words but he heard them—felt them—as if she'd screamed them. His damned imagination fed him a fantasy. He kissed her. Silencing himself. Taking control. Because now he regretted asking. Now he *wanted*...the impossible. He could not do anything with this. All he could do was hold her now. Drive closer now. As close as he could—over and over—until in the fiery fury of his desperation she came. Her cry pierced his heart. Her violent convulsions of pleasure almost milked his.

He growled—pulling out enough to retain control. Because he was not done yet. This night could never be over so quick.

Not when it was all he had left.

CHAPTER ELEVEN

ARES GLARED OUT of the window, ignoring the calming tea cooling on the table behind him. He counted but it was an exercise in pure futility. The pain in his chest hadn't just returned, but was bigger than ever. Once more he regulated his breathing, trying to loosen the crushed sensation, yet the vice-like grip beneath his ribs only tightened. It didn't matter if he counted to four or forty. This was different—not a stress attack from too much coffee and too many hours of work. This was sheer *dread*. He never should have touched her again.

I've only ever had you.

Possessive triumph raged through his blood as her broken admission echoed in his brain—a satisfaction he had no right to feel. Because the flip side hit less than a second later—a burning devastation that smacked him down. *Why* hadn't she met someone else? Hell, he almost wished she had. Because now he knew she didn't understand the reality—that by staying with him, she was accepting *less* than what she could have had. Now he realised that her choice this week—to let him in again—hadn't been an *informed* decision. He'd thought she'd lived a little more of life and, sure, in several ways she had. She'd held her own with the elite at last night's party and he knew she would thrive—beautifully—in any kind of society now. Not because she was in any way better than before. She was as kind and as strong and as wonderful—it was simply that she actually believed it now.

She was so much more confident than when they'd first met. Since then she'd grieved for her grandmother, found a new family of friends and built a career she loved... The *problem* was she was still naïve when it came to men. To relationships. To *him*. He'd never been *fully* honest with her. He'd never admitted his limitations—while she'd bloomed, he still lacked. And for all her flourishing, she'd not learned what *more* she might have from someone else so she hadn't consciously *chosen* the less he offered. And the fact was, he could never be all she really wanted or needed.

The first time round he'd assumed he could be fairly absent and it wouldn't matter. She would live on the island where she'd been vibrantly happy. He could keep her—and any children—safely away from his family of vipers. He'd go at weekends so he'd be close enough but not too intimate. Good sex but minimal emotional impact. He'd thought that it could stay light and easy. She would have a warm home with space for her art where she could love her children and teach them to sail...

But her doubts were raised the second she'd heard Gia's ludicrous suggestion that he'd only married her to avoid the pressure to marry Sophia. Or maybe she'd already had doubts, given she'd barely trusted him enough to ask for his side of the story—rather she'd asked only the one direct question.

Do you love me?

The stark misery in her eyes had savaged him. Already twisted up by being at the damned compound, by his cousins' watchfulness and Gia's stupid games, he'd not been able to answer. Certainly not the way she'd wanted. And because she was stronger than he'd realised then, she'd run. She'd been right to.

She was even stronger now. That meant she would fight him today. It was also why he had to win. Because his wife deserved to be with someone who offered more than money and nice houses and good sex only at the weekends. He'd not realised how badly the prospect of his absence had hurt her. But now he understood that she'd grown up with her father often away and she didn't want that for herself again. Or for her children. Bethan today wouldn't just ask for more, she would *demand* it. As she should. But that 'more' was something he couldn't ever give.

And even if she chose to stay now, ultimately she would leave again. Again, as she should. But he wouldn't survive losing her then.

Only now could he admit to himself how bad it had been last time. He'd buried his anger in ice but with her coming back this week, it had melted. At its core was pure pain from her absolute rejection that day. And it was still raw. He'd failed his mother and couldn't ever make it right. He couldn't fail Bethan again. Certainly never any children. He couldn't hurt *her* children in that way. He wasn't emotionally equipped to be what they needed. So he needed to follow through on his promise now.

He needed space. He needed to be alone. He would be again.

* * *

Bethan paused in the doorway of the lounge and braced. Ares stood stiffly by the window, framed by the brilliant blue sky, his dark three-piece suit a masterclass in formality. He didn't just have those metaphorical walls up, he was in full armour.

'I've filed the paperwork and made my declaration,' he said the second he turned and saw her. 'Theo will take you to your lawyer and then to make your filing. He'll then take you to the airport.'

Bethan breathed through the impact of verbal hit after hit. She'd known he could be ruthless but she'd not expected him to be quite *this* cold. Not after last night. It hadn't just been amazing, surely it had changed everything?

No. He still wanted to end their marriage. Still wanted her to *leave*. He didn't want her in his life long-term. How was that possible when last night—when this whole week—they'd *shared*—so much more than their bodies? When she'd fallen for him all over again only even deeper this time because this time they'd truly talked and now she understood—?

'This is what's best for you, Bethan.'

'No, this is what *you* want,' she flared at his patronising tone.

She didn't believe him. She *couldn't*—

'I need to go.' He glanced at his watch. 'I have meetings.'

So he could spare only a few seconds to slice her from his life? Was he really going to leave without talking this through? He'd just made a stupid snap decision and now they both had to live with it?

She refused to move, suddenly realising that was what *she'd* done last time. She'd flipped out and walked. Was this payback for her doing that? Or was talking more pointless because he really didn't care?

No. They *wanted* each other. They were dynamite together. And now they knew and understood each other so much more so she wasn't going anywhere. *She* would stay and fight this time.

'So you're leaving because you don't want…' She trailed off expectantly, forcing him to explain why.

His nostrils thinned, somehow he stood taller and straighter but she was right in his way unless he picked her up and set her to the side. He didn't. He shoved his hands deeper into his pockets and glared at her.

'You deserve better.' He ground out the most clichéd brush-off ever.

Bethan stepped closer and summoned more courage. 'I don't want better,' she said softly. 'I just want you. All I've ever really wanted was you. Just you.'

Desperately nervous, she gazed into his face, trying to read his reaction. But there was none. It wasn't that he'd assumed his cool expressionless mask—he was simply deadened. Hollow. He shook his head, crushing her bravado without so much as a word. Her brain turned sluggish. Everything seemed to be happening weirdly slowly.

'Why?' she whispered.

He closed his eyes briefly. 'I can't give you what you want.'

'What do you *think* I want?' she muttered. 'What else is there?'

She'd just said she only wanted *him*. None of the

fancy things others expected of him. She didn't give a damn about dollars or properties or how many people he was in charge of. She just wanted to be *with* him.

'Children.'

Rigid, she stared at the bleakness in his eyes and *refused* to breathe. 'You don't want children?'

'And you want love,' he added hoarsely. 'You *deserve* love.'

Pain whistled through her and she found herself asking again—a variant on the question that had caused her so much heartache already. 'And you can't give me that?'

'Not the kind you deserve.' He folded his arms across his chest. 'When we married I thought you'd be happy on the island. That if we had children, they'd be there with you. I would only be there on the weekends. Now I know that wouldn't be enough for you but I can't offer more.'

He'd wanted to compartmentalise—his home life, his work. He'd wanted to keep her away from the Vasiliadis compound back then, not because there was something wrong with her, but with his family. Now she understood the loneliness and pressure he'd endured there, she could see why he'd wanted to protect her.

Had it been more? Had he wanted her to be his sanctuary—to be at that villa like his safe haven? So why then would he want to see her so little? Would he really have been happy to share her bed for only a couple of nights a week? Maybe all he'd wanted was for her to give him heirs so he'd carry on that damned Vasiliadis lineage, while he lived it up in Athens with affairs?

No. Ares was faithful to the bone. He would never do that. And he was so damned determinedly independent. So hope wouldn't die within her.

'Why can't you be with me all the time?' she pressed. 'Why did you really want that distance?'

His face paled but his gaze didn't waver from hers. 'I can't be an involved father,' he muttered.

'Because…?' She waited.

In the long silence her brain fired up, desperately searching for reasons in the face of his compressed mouth.

'You don't want to be like yours was? Because you never had a decent example… Is that why?' she asked.

He finally broke from her gaze and bowed his head and didn't deny it.

His father hadn't just been absent, he'd rejected his role altogether. While his grandfather had been a bully. Ares would be so much better than either of those men—surely he *knew* that? She frantically tried to think of solutions—straining to convince him. 'You know I've never had an example of a real working relationship—only the romantic, idealistic memories my father fed me, and my grandmother. But that doesn't mean I can't *learn* how to get through the complexities of marriage. You could learn with me.'

He was so very still. 'I'm not able to do that, Bethan.'

'Because you don't want to,' she breathed. He didn't want her enough.

'Because I can't give you the lifestyle with the kind of family you want,' he reiterated.

'Because you don't want to *be* there—not all the time. You really think you're incapable of that?'

He clenched his fists. 'I'm not going to stand in the way of your dreams.'

'You really think ending this is what's best for me?'

'Yes. I want what's best for you, Bethan. I like you.'

Like. Not *love*. It punched. But she didn't believe him.

'Yet you made love to me last night.' Rebellious—resentful—she lifted her chin in the face of his icy demeanour. 'That is what you did, Ares. And I made love right back to you.'

'We both knew it was the last time,' he said flatly. 'That's why it felt…'

She waited but he didn't finish. She could guess the rest anyway—why it felt *special*.

He was wrong. He was grasping for reasons to push her away. The problem was she now hurt too much to be able to think—too confused and flustered to fight effectively.

'Just go to the lawyer now,' he ordered harshly. 'The divorce should be processed in less than a fortnight. I need to go to work.' He strode past her.

She didn't try to block him. There was no stopping Ares when he was this determined but her words escaped anyway in a final futile attempt.

'You're running away. You're a coward.'

He paused but didn't turn to face her. 'I'm sorry, Bethan. I can't be what you want.'

CHAPTER TWELVE

BETHAN SAT BY the garret window and pulled the small trolley nearer her table. There was nothing better than work. Particularly painstaking, fine-detailed, miniature-scale work that took every ounce of her concentration and dexterity. It was the only balm that could soothe her tortured brain. She worked—long hours, late nights. When she got home she worked on other projects. Phoebe was going to have to birth octuplets to utilise all the baby blankets Bethan had knitted for her in this desperate surge of productivity. Despite working until her eyes and arms ached, she couldn't sleep. Could only overthink. Only yearn. Only grow angrier. Her eyes were tired and sore—from working, not crying. She glanced out of the window yet again to rest them. Not so secretly hoping to see Ares striding along the footpath. She never did.

I chase after no one.

He hadn't before. He wouldn't now. She just needed to get over him. She'd arrived back in London to find Phoebe had gone abroad—working on things with the father of her baby—while Elodie also was away. It was actually good to have some time to process it internally before trying to talk to them. As there was a new manager for the escape room, Bethan was free to quietly work on various props plus her personal pieces from the small studio she had on the top floor of the central London building. She would rebuild her life. She was lunching later in the week with Elodie's sister, Ashleigh—she would *not* be wrecked for ever. She'd survived this once and she would survive it again. Only this time she was more furious. This time she understood so much more. The man was *bone-headed*. Stubbornly isolating himself when he didn't have to and denying them both *everything*.

Yes, *she'd* been a romantic but that didn't mean she'd been *all* wrong. Love healed. Humans craved company and community and they needed it. She had changed—some—in the years they'd been apart. She'd gone from shy and awkwardly babbling to confidently keeping her counsel. *Thinking* before speaking. Thinking before *doing*. Though she'd lost all that progress the second she'd faced Ares again. He got to her like no one else. He *mattered* like no one else. And she wanted to love him. But he didn't want that.

He hadn't run away from the expectations and the pressure of the Vasiliadis family. He'd fought his way to the top—not to take power and control, not even to get his revenge, but because beneath it all he'd ached for their acceptance. And never gotten it.

She'd offered him more than acceptance. She'd offered him her heart. Unconditionally. Of course it mightn't be easy because they each had baggage but they could—would—be amazing. But he wasn't willing to risk whatever heart he had left.

* * *

Ares sipped the scalding coffee. There wasn't a pain in his chest any more. It wasn't hard to breathe. There wasn't a constant sense of impending terror. Honestly, there was nothing. He was hollow. And it was good.

Four days had passed since he'd walked out. Theo had driven her to the lawyer, she'd made her declaration, the required paperwork had been filed. She'd boarded the first commercial flight, rejecting the offer of Ares's private jet. All her things were cleared from his Athens apartment and it shouldn't be long before he received the divorce decree.

Filled with his restless, boundless energy of old he worked—able to sustain long hours easily as he had before. The source was cold rage. It had served him well for so long and he was on a roll. He would go to the villa at the weekend. Going back there would only confirm that he'd done the right thing. He would reclaim it as he already had the apartment. Exorcise the ghost of her for good.

But when the helicopter landed on Avra a few days later, he had to brace. There were more than memories here, there were *things*...

Or there had been. Stunned, Ares walked from the bedroom to the studio to the lounge. *Everything* of hers was gone—the things he'd bought her, the things she'd made, the tools and supplies. The only thing that remained was the sculpture he'd bought at the auction. He phoned Theo, who explained that she'd asked for everything—her clothes and supplies—to be boxed up and donated. *Donated.*

'You've done it so quickly.' Ares absently rubbed the

hollow in his chest as he glanced around the spotless, empty studio.

'Should we not have?' Theo sounded worried. 'I can—'

'It's fine. You did as she asked, which was correct. Thank you.'

There was a rubber band on the table, but no knot in the middle of it. No scraps of this or that. No more balls of yarn tucked about the place. In less than a week she'd filled the villa with projects in varying states of completion but now all remnants of them were gone.

He went outside to the bins and lifted the lids. They'd been emptied already. His staff were that efficient. But at the very bottom he saw a couple of threads. Wool the colour of the kind she'd bound him to bed with on the boat.

She'd gotten rid of everything he'd given her. He released a long sigh and leaned against the wall of the house as that endless rage suddenly and completely evaporated. Exhaustion hit. Instant and crippling. He sank to the ground. It wasn't his chest that hurt, but everything. The inescapable, bone-deep ache intensified. The flu, no?

He dragged himself inside. Fell onto the bed. Spent twenty-four hours wrapped in blankets. But there was no fever, only that ache. The erosion of his control was complete, leaving him facing the endless reality of being utterly alone.

On the third morning he made himself get up. No more wallowing, he had work to do. He skimmed the million messages, replied to only the most essential— mainly to tell his PA to instruct everyone that he was on leave. Then he walked down to the beach. Fresh air would do the trick.

He took the boat out—puttered around to the village harbour where he'd dropped her that first day. He never should have given her the ride but he'd been unable to resist. The boat bumped against the concrete dock and Ares winced. He jumped to secure the line, making an uncharacteristic hash of it when he became aware of a shadow. Someone was watching. He spun, heart pounding. But it wasn't Bethan. It was a young boy.

'You've not done it right.' The boy stared at the mangled rope.

'Yeah,' Ares chuckled weakly.

The boy moved forward and swiftly retied the line. Securely. He straightened, looking up. 'You're Ares Vasiliadis.'

'I am.'

The boy's eyes widened. 'You're training crew for those fancy boats.'

'Future deckhands. Captains. Yeah.'

The boy shot the fixed line a sideways look and Ares grinned.

'I'm just providing the money,' he added.

'I can sail. I'm fast.'

'I bet.' Ares nodded.

'Niko!' A woman hurried down the path. As she approached, recognition changed her demeanour. 'You're Ares—'

'Vasiliadis, yes. Niko helped secure my boat. When he's a bit older he should apply to the Melina Foundation, he's got skills, could be a fine sailor one day.'

Niko grew about a foot in front of them.

His mother smiled. 'His grandfather's a fisherman.'

'So it's in the blood, then.' Ares managed a smile back and headed up the path with a nod of farewell.

You're good with them.

Bethan had enjoyed his banter with the trainees on *Artemis*. Honestly, he'd enjoyed spending time with them. He'd liked Niko just now too—his guileless curiosity, his instinctive interest and confidence. Ares's own instinct was to want the best for him—as he'd wanted for the trainees too. And that boy was a complete stranger. If he had his *own* children he would want more than the best for them, he would do anything to help, to protect, to love them. He'd want to be *with* them.

Pain struck his chest as if someone had shoved a poisoned lance into his ribs and impaled his heart. He abandoned the steep path and turned back. It took double the usual time to boat back to the villa.

In the lounge he stared at her sculpture. If he still had that energy, if he still had that rage, he would take that hammer she'd found and smash it himself. But there was no energy. No rage. Only the ache that was now worsening by the second. She'd used all kinds of items to create it—taking broken threads and weaving them together—marrying other items to make something new. Something beautiful. She'd even brought him and Gia together for a brief moment.

He sank onto the sofa. He'd not been able to handle Bethan's calm dignity, her kind reason delivered with *compassion*. But now he saw—through the pain, to the truth. God, he *had* been a coward.

He'd let her think the worst. Fobbed her off with a weak excuse. He'd been too scared to tell her that *he was too scared*. He was screwed up and so he *had* screwed up the most important thing to enter his life.

He was supposedly successful. He could have anything money could buy. He'd taken the reins of an enormous company and built it even bigger. But the fact was he felt like rubbish inside. He felt unlovable. Unwilling to risk letting someone in for fear they found out the truth. That there was a reason why his father had never wanted to acknowledge him. A reason why his mother had forced him to live with people who'd barely accepted his existence—why she'd rejected him the moment she'd had the chance. The Vasiliadis family were broken—driven by greed and a rapacious need for power. They'd wanted his blood lineage, his brain and branded an insane work ethic into him. But they'd not actually wanted *him*. They *tolerated* him, but so unwillingly. They'd only paid attention when he'd proved himself the way they required—with financial success. But he was broken too. His endless rage sprang from that bottomless well of rejection—because he'd not been wanted from the start.

Except that wasn't *quite* true. His mother had wanted him. She'd *kept* him, cared for him and worked so hard to provide for them both. In the early years she'd refused to give him up, even when she'd had no support from family of her own, let alone Loukas Vasiliadis. Ares remembered those days when she'd not had a shift and she'd taken him to the beach. She'd taught him to swim, to sail. She *had* loved him. He knew that her sending him to the Vasiliadis compound had been born from some desperate belief that he would have a better life than she could provide. She'd just not given him any choice in that decision. She'd known he'd not wanted to go, so she'd lied to make him.

Which was exactly what he'd done to Bethan.

He'd pushed her away. Let her leave believing a lie. But him denying them a relationship wasn't what was best for *her*. He'd been trying to protect himself. Because he had the biggest fear of failure on earth. Of rejection. He'd not explained to her about it years ago—he'd been stressed and gone cold and she'd misinterpreted his silence. He'd valued actions over words but he'd failed her in both departments. Both back then and now.

Because the irony was *Bethan* had valued him. She'd appreciated, not just his body, but his humour—the humour that emerged only with her. Because she was sweet and funny. And safe. And she appreciated his attempt to honour his mother. He wanted to take her boating again. Wanted to take their babies too—he would teach them to swim and sail. Bethan would teach them how to tie firm knots because securing connections—*caring*—was what she was so good at. And she'd truly cared for him.

Bethan was the one person in his life who'd told him he should be proud of himself. So maybe, if he was fully honest with her—she might be right.

CHAPTER THIRTEEN

BETHAN WEAVED ALONG the busy footpath, that prickling sensation down her spine worsening. She'd met Ashleigh at a cafe only ten minutes from the escape room and indulged in a ninety-minute lunch. Hearing about Ashleigh's study, about Elodie's travels and sharing news about Phoebe, who was now back in Italy, was the perfect distraction from her circuitous thoughts. And from the devastation of opening a courier package this morning and finding her divorce decree inside. She was officially, legally single. She and Ares were done.

She'd not told Ashleigh. She'd just arranged to meet her for lunch again in a week. She was going to a theatre show tonight and a gallery exhibition later in a few days. All with work contacts. Work was everything. It was how she would survive.

But before getting to the door she glanced around. She'd noticed the enormous SUV with tinted windows parked across the street from the cafe but dismissed it. Now the same vehicle was idling opposite the escape room entrance. No way would it be him—that idea was a mere weak-moment wish. But her gut tightened, forcing her to check. She stomped straight across the road, pacing in time to her thudding heart. As she neared, the rear passenger window slid down. Grey-blue eyes raked over her. Stubble shadowed a particularly sharp jaw. Bethan glared into his drawn—still devastating—features. Seriously? Today of all days?

'Are you following me?' she growled through the window.

'I didn't want to interrupt you,' he said tightly. 'I wanted to wait 'til—'

'When?' she queried furiously. 'Until when, exactly? What do you actually need before you can—?' She broke off, breathless.

And this was pointless. They were done. The decree proved it. But just as she backed away, he opened the door, grabbed her arm and tugged. She tumbled, sprawling onto the back seat. She heard the door thud and a rapid instruction in Greek. One she understood. *Move.*

'What are you doing?' she demanded, scraping herself up and into the corner as far from him as possible. 'Ares!'

'Put your seat belt on,' he said.

'What?' She gaped.

His cheeks were flushed and his breathing was visibly jerky but he grabbed the strap from behind her shoulder and fastened it around her—the action bringing him so close she could smell him. She only need lean an inch forward to brush—

'You need to be safe,' he said roughly.

'Stalking me and kidnapping me off the street is your idea of *safe*?'

He leaned back and jammed his own seat belt home.

'I'll stop the car if you want, but I hope you'll hear what I have to say first.'

Bethan's brain fuzzed. What could he possibly want to say? And she did *not* want to be in an enclosed space with him. The driver was Ares's employee and behind a screen and didn't count as a normal functioning human in this arena. She glanced away as her heart skipped too many beats to supply her brain with anywhere near like enough power.

'Say *what*, Ares?' she prompted. 'Hurry up and spit it out.'

Silence. Three counts. Four. Was he counting? Because she was. She made it to seven before—

'Bethan,' he muttered softly.

She closed her eyes against that thread of humour, that rich vein of temptation. The whisper she'd never been able to resist. And in the end that magnetism was still too much. Cursing her weakness, she looked at him. He was fully focused on her. She blinked, noting other details to dilute the impact of those stormy eyes. His hair was ruffled, his complexion paler than normal, his jaw-line even more sculpted as if he was gritting his teeth. He didn't look as if he'd been sleeping well. Didn't look as if he'd been working much either, given he wasn't in a suit but jeans and an old tee. It was grey—highlighting the slate blue of his eyes—the tee he'd been wearing the day they'd met. She didn't want to believe that was deliberate, but there was that swirling, raw emotion in his eyes.

'I love you,' he said.

Time froze. So did she. Didn't want to decide whether what she'd heard was real or not.

'I love you, Bethan.' Not a sweet whisper but a husky, broken declaration.

Still she couldn't breathe. Or believe. But those three words sank like little stones deep inside.

He suddenly leaned towards her until the belt jerked and held him back. 'I love you.' He rushed on. 'I am absolutely, utterly, completely in love with you and I know there's so much more I need to say but first I just need you to know I love you.'

But it was too late. They were divorced. Their marriage was dead.

'Ares.' To her horror she couldn't get her voice above a pitiful mewl. 'Don't… I can't…' She couldn't survive losing him again. 'We're done. The divorce…'

'Came through. I know. And I'm so sorry.'

Devastated, she could only stare at him as tears filled her eyes.

His expression pinched. 'The thing about being driven at speed is we have to stay in our seats, belted up, right? Can't touch. Because my problem is I can't resist touching you. My first instinct is to touch you, take you, keep you close. It's what I always want to do when you're near. But I've not been great at opening up about why. About anything, really. But right now I can't touch you how I want because this car is moving—'

'You're saying you need to be physically restrained around me?'

A memory fragment hit—of her binding his wrists, of him letting her do as she pleased with him. The playfulness they'd shared had masked a deeper resonance. A spark flickered in his eyes as if he too had been struck by the same recollection.

'Pretty much.' He breathed deeply again. 'It's always easier—more impactful—to show than tell, but I've not been showing you everything. Not how truly I love you.'

Those words—three more little stones—sank deep and settled with the others.

'I'm sorry to have caused you more heartbreak. You've lost enough already.' His expression softened. 'I've realised I have some baggage. What happened with my parents left me feeling unwanted... It struck deep. I guess that feeling...fear...led me to make some bad decisions, but I'm trying to work through it because I want to start over with you.'

Start over *how*? Bethan stared. Not interrupting, needing to hear *all* he had to say because surely this was impossible.

'You're a beautiful person, Bethan,' he muttered. 'You believe in good things and that's never something to apologise for. I think that's a gift. You believed in me when I didn't. And when I didn't deserve it. You were brave enough to be honest with me but I wasn't as brave with you.' He swallowed. 'The other day I let you leave thinking all sorts of stupid things. Like that I couldn't love you. It was easier than being honest, but it was awfully cruel to you.' He bent his head and his voice thinned. 'I pushed you away with lies.'

Lies. Her heart pounded.

'My mother did that to me all those years ago when she said I was a burden. I have to hope she genuinely believed me going to Grandfather was in my best interests. But when I pushed you, it wasn't really because I thought it would be best for you. It was because I couldn't believe that the best *person* I'd ever met could ever truly want me.' He paused. 'At least not for long.'

Bethan shrank deeper into her seat, hurt that he'd not trusted her yet able to understand why. Because he'd been hurt by a level of rejection she'd never imagined before, let alone had to endure.

'When we first married, you found out I wanted you to live at the villa. You thought I didn't want to have you in Athens during the week but you understand now that my life there was only work, no? There was never—would never be—anyone else.'

Every muscle was so stiff her nod was a jerk.

He breathed out, leaned closer. 'It wasn't that I wanted to hide you away. I thought if I wasn't there all the time, it would take longer for you to realise I'm not... That it would take longer for you not to want me any more.' A strained half-smile briefly broke through his tension. 'I haven't felt wanted for me—just *me*—for a really long time.'

If ever, right? Bethan's heart just broke. He'd been so wary he'd never let anyone that close.

'I need to be more honest,' he said. 'The truth is I loved the idea of you being in the villa. I was super possessive and wanted to know you were there waiting for me. Only for me. Always for me. That you were safe and no one could take you away. That you were mine. If I'm really honest, that's *still* what I dream of. But now I want to live there with you. Not leaving after only a couple of nights. Knowing for sure that you would never send me away. That you would always want me to stay. That's what I really want. That's my dream.' He was actually sweating now. 'Is that awfully selfish of me?'

'Oh, Ares.' What he wanted was everything she wanted too.

'I'm terrified, Bethan. I screwed up and I don't really know how to fix this other than to tell you that I was a fool and I'm sorry and you deserve so much better but if you'll give me one last chance, I'll show you. I'll tell you. I'll—'

'You know I wanted you when I thought you were an ordinary guy working on a tiny ferry,' she interrupted fiercely. 'I never wanted your billions or your beastly family connections.'

'I know.' That smallest smile quirked his lips. 'You wanted my body.'

'You wanted mine,' she countered. 'But not only did I want your body, you were kind. You went out of your way to help me. You gave me water. A hat. A ride on your boat even when it wasn't your job. Even when you really didn't want to.'

'Oh, I wanted to.'

'Because you're kind.'

He paused. 'Only to you.'

'That's good enough for me.' She cocked her head as his lips twisted. 'And not quite true. You were nice to those trainees. You let me see *you* that day, Ares. And I wanted you just for you.'

'Bethan.' His voice cracked. 'I love you.'

Each time he said it, that pile of stones inside her grew—becoming a foundation on which all hope, all future could be built. And she realised that he needed it too—that rock of certainty inside. He'd never had it and she could gladly give him that.

'I share your dream, Ares,' she admitted in a heartfelt tumble of truth. 'I want to share life—*everything*—with you. And I will until I die. Because I love you too. So much.'

But instead of matching her smile, his expression crumpled. 'I've been so stupid. I should have come after you when you left me back then. God, I've wasted so much time.' He dropped his head into his hands. 'I didn't understand how much you meant to me until after I brought you back to Greece and we actually communicated beyond the bedroom. I've been blind and stubborn.'

'I've been every bit as stubborn.' She nudged his chin so he met her eyes again. 'And maybe I needed that time, Ares,' she whispered. 'I needed to figure myself out. Needed to grieve properly and grow as a person so I could be an equal partner for you. Because you're crazy strong and capable. It took so much to push all that hurt down and hold it together all on your own for so long. But you don't have to any more. I'm here. I can handle it. I can handle you. And I know you can handle me. So you can let me in now. This is our time—we're together, right when we're meant to be.'

'You're too generous.' He reached for her but was stopped by the snap of the seat belt again. He muttered a curse. 'Can I please unfasten your seat belt now?'

She'd completely forgotten they were driving. Shocked, she looked out of the window and saw, not only had they stopped, but they were parked in a garage.

'Where are we?' She peered forward but couldn't see much in the dimness. 'Where's the driver?'

'Probably inside the house.'

'What house?' But she knew already. 'You've bought a house here in London?'

'I'll show it to you soon.' He nodded, releasing his seat belt. 'We can move if you don't like it, but I wanted a base so I can...maybe take you to dinner.'

'You want to take me to dinner?' A small chuckle escaped.

He pushed the button on her seat belt. 'Every night.'

His hands were firm on her waist and he pulled her close in a smooth, powerful move. His lips were on hers and their tears, their tongues mingled. It was messy and beautiful and dark and safe. So safe. The kisses deepened and slowly, so slowly, Bethan believed.

'Bethan, darling. You're so beautiful. I'm so sorry. Can we start over?'

For a moment she rested her forehead on his shoulder and he gently combed her hair back with his fingers.

'Dinner, you say?' she murmured.

'To start. I guess maybe we should take it slower this time.'

'Should we?' Bethan wriggled—basically crawled onto his lap. 'Not that much slower.'

She needed to be close to him. Needed to love him. She just needed *him*.

His arms swept about her. 'Damn, Bethan,' he groaned as she wrapped herself around him. 'The last couple of weeks have been the roughest of my life and there have been some rough ones.'

'Me too,' she whispered.

'I've missed you so much,' he muttered.

Bethan wasn't taking anything slow now. She dug into his jeans pocket. Chuckling when she found the protection. 'You were confident,' she teased as she drew it out.

'Hopeful. Desperate, actually. Love you so much.'

She was every bit as desperate. Aching and impatient, they kissed and fumbled clothing aside just enough to prepare him, to bare her. Gasping, she sank onto him as he filled her in that way that only he could. This was *everything* and so overwhelming her tears streamed.

'I thought I'd never have this again. Never have you again,' she sobbed.

'I know. I'm here now. I'll always be here for you,' he crooned, holding her closer, soothing her with whispers of love as he took her back to slow—so slow they were barely moving. *'I love you. I love you. I love you.'* Tenderly sealed together as he whispered it over and over, turning tears to happiness to pure truth.

Inexorably the compulsion to ride him faster grew. His touches became teases and ultimately exquisite torture as he devoured her. His face flushed as he cupped her breasts, scraped his teeth over one nipple then licked the other. He spread his hands wide over her hips to help her rise and fall on him. She loved how much he enjoyed her softness—as she loved the powerful hardness of him. They worked together, rubbing in the best possible way.

'You're the best thing ever to walk into my life.' He nuzzled her neck. 'I couldn't comprehend it at the time. Couldn't believe it. You bring everything I never thought I could have. Could never admit that I even wanted. You're absolutely everything to me.'

She heard the tremble in his voice, felt him shaking beneath her, knew just how much he needed *her*. Not just to know, but to *believe*. He needed that same foundation as she. So she wrapped her arms and legs about him even more tightly.

'I'm not going to let you go,' she whispered fiercely. 'Never. You're mine, Ares. You'll always be mine.'

'Yes.' He clutched her hard as ecstasy overwhelmed them both. *'Yes.'*

Slowly the warm silence morphed—from breathless, to content, to utterly dreamy. She lifted her head and smiled at him. The tired strain around his eyes had evaporated. He was her gorgeous, vital Ares again. And he smiled back.

'Afternoon sex suits you,' she chuckled.

'Making love with *you*—any time and every time—suits me.' He kissed her. 'I'm giving you fair warning, Bethan.'

'Warning for what?'

'Believing in a full and happy future isn't a fantasy. We can have what your parents and grandparents had—a happy, loving marriage. So I'm warning you that I'm going to ask you to marry me again. I love you and I want to spend the rest of my life with you—in Athens, here in London, at the villa—wherever work or whim takes us. I want to be with you, build a family, have *everything*—the downs as well as the ups—we'll face them together, no?'

He was offering her everything with the confidence that came, not from holding secrets and shame back, but from sharing all their feelings and fears.

'Sounds like paradise to me.' She melted.

He smiled at her again—happiness glinting with renewed desire. 'I know you need time, but I will ask and I will keep asking for as long as it takes…'

'Ares.' She cupped his face between her palms, her smile tremulous and her heart soaring. 'When have I ever been able to say anything other than yes to you?'

CHAPTER FOURTEEN

Three years later

ARES WATCHED BETHAN adjust her display. A tiny tweak here, removal of an invisible speck there. He knew she worried it was too soon for a solo exhibition, but she was more than ready, she was gifted. Already the title cards of several pieces bore the discreet mark signifying they'd been sold and the pre-show reviews had reassured her. Ares had delighted in quoting extracts from one at regular intervals during her preparations today—

Bethan's mixed media work intersects fine art and traditional craft. The intricacy of her beadwork, the ethereal light of her ceramics, the precision of needlework and the dexterity of her brushstrokes all illustrate her command of a breathtaking plethora of techniques. Beyond brimming with skill, talent, and clever concepts, Bethan transcends her virtuosity and demands an emotional response—

She certainly drew an emotional response from him. Especially wearing that blue-grey silk dress that clung to her body like water and was the colour of his eyes. God, he loved her in it.

He caught her close and murmured in her ear. 'You transcend, Bethan.'

Chuckling, she turned towards him, colour blooming in her cheeks. 'I do okay.'

'So much more than okay.'

He released her as the first guests arrived. She stepped away, gleaming in the centre of the sublimely lit gallery. It was a rarefied space in the heart of the exclusive central London hotel that her friend Elodie's husband owned. And of course, it was her friends who'd arrived first. He watched her embrace them, basking in the glow of her beauty, confidence, kindness and quietly exulted in the knowledge that at the end of the night she would return to him. Always she would return to him. Just as he would always wait for her. Though he felt impatience tease as he scoped the sweep and fall of the silk about her body. He was *very* much looking forward to the night ahead. Happily they were staying right here in the hotel, which meant less than a three-minute walk and elevator ride to a bed. He couldn't wait to free her curves from that fabric.

They'd re-married less than a year after their divorce—on their beach again but this time her friends had been there, plus Sophia and Felipe. Even Gia had accepted the invitation. Ares found he cared less about the past—he had contentment *now*. And security. He knew *who* he was and, while he needed to honour and remember his mother, he'd also begun to accept that maybe his father could be—if not forgiven—at least a little understood. Growing up in the Vasiliadis compound with Pavlos would damage anyone. Ares had the capacity to realise that now there was an abundance of love in his heart. The love Bethan gave him. She gave and he grew and delighted in giving back and somehow it grew between them even more. Limitless, joyous, so very easy. She'd changed his life completely.

Bethan sidled towards the rear of the room, needing a quiet moment to power up before more socialising with prospective customers. She sipped *lemonada* from a champagne glass, stifling a giggle as she watched Elodie glide about the room. She was so glad her friends were here. Elodie's fiery hair, together with the beaded bustier Bethan had made for her years ago, caught the light—sparking an idea for a new creative piece. Phoebe floated alongside Elodie, proclaiming her delight about enjoying a glamorous night out as if she didn't fly around the world attending opera and exclusive events on a regular basis. Both her friends' babies were safely asleep just upstairs, attended by their highly experienced, highly paid nannies.

Sophia Dimou arrived, immediately gravitating through the throng to the two high-spirited women. Felipe followed, turning to the two men watching them. It turned out that, aside from the Vasiliadis connection, Felipe was a business associate of Phoebe's husband, Eduardo. Reputation would have the world believe all three of those men were ruthless tycoons, but right now they seemed somewhat helpless—captivated by the vivacious feminine trio. In moments the men joined them and the atmosphere bubbled higher.

That they'd all come tonight was infinitely precious

to her. Truthfully, it wasn't her own success that moved her, but seeing those she loved most in the world together and so very happy. She searched the crowd for Ares, only to find him already looking right at her from the farthest corner. His mouth curved in that tender, knowing smile that was hers alone. Despite the distance—the forty people standing between them—she felt his love wrapping around her. And his love—entwined with that of her friends—was overwhelming.

Blinking quickly, she turned away and slipped out of the nearest exit. She needed more than a quiet moment to compose herself. She sniffed and hurried to the elevator. Ridiculous—to be teary because she was so totally happy? She needed to get a grip before she wrecked her make-up. She had to address that entire room soon.

As the elevator chimed, a big hand engulfed hers, his thumb rubbing over the rings she wore—the diamond had been reset to fit and form a knot together with the ruby of their second engagement—their past not forgotten, but celebrated.

'Surely you're not running away?' he teased.

'I just need to get myself together before I have to talk.'

'Want some company?' He tugged her into the lift and wrapped his arms around her.

She closed her eyes and leaned into the hug, feeling his heart beat steadily beneath her cheek. This wasn't doing her make-up any favours, or making her any less emotional, but it didn't matter. She was what she was and all those people downstairs supported her, not in spite of, but because of her emotionality.

When the elevator opened, Ares led the way, not speaking again until they were inside their hotel suite.

'Anything I can do to help?' His gaze roamed over her features intently.

He already was helping and her heart simply burst.

She sniffled, then dragged in a deep breath. 'Actually there is something else I'd like to make…'

'Oh?' His smile turned sinful. 'You want me to make—'

'A baby with me. Yes.'

'Bethan,' he said slowly, so husky. 'I would love to do that with you.'

Her eyes filled and as she nodded her tears splashed. 'Good. Thank you. *Please.*'

'Right now?' He tenderly swiped his thumbs beneath her eyes to stop more falling 'Sweetheart,' he breathed. 'You're supposed to be giving a speech in half an hour.'

'I don't care.' She sniffed. 'Okay, I do care.' Her eyes filled again. 'About everything.'

He leaned close, all reassurance and strength. 'You're going to nail it.'

'Yeah.' She giggled through her tears. 'Because you're going to nail me now.'

'Beautiful Bethan, I love you. And I will do anything you want.' He walked her backwards to the bed, gathering her skirt in his hands as he went—bunching it up and over her curvy hips to her waist.

'You're *sure*?' She needed to check.

'Never more sure of anything. I can't wait to make our family bigger.' He swept his hand across her lower belly. 'You think now might be a good time?'

'Literally. I started tracking my cycle and…' She

couldn't finish her sentence as he ran his finger along the inside leg of her panties, hooked the elastic and tugged them down, dropping to his knees as he did.

Just being near him made her melt and when he looked at her like this, when he touched her like this... *always* he set her alight.

'I...uh...' She trailed off as he pushed her to sit on the edge of the bed.

He pushed her knees apart. 'Let me get you ready—'

'I am ready...' she moaned.

There was no point arguing with him and honestly? She was the winner here.

He swept his palms up the inside of her thighs and followed their path with his mouth. 'The more orgasms you have, the more likely you are to conceive.'

'Is that an actual scientific fact?' She giggled, arching into his touch.

'It is in my world.' A husky, hot whisper before he mouthed her—

'I...guess I can...uh...'

'Come on me.'

'Yeeeeahhhh...' Pleasure rippled as she rode his fingers, his tongue whipping her higher with a devilish dance. So easily he coaxed her to climax.

'Ares, *love me*,' she whispered brokenly, needing him inside her. Now.

'I am loving you, darling, I always will.' Gently he lifted her, setting her on all fours near the edge of the bed. 'And as much as I want to smother your face in kisses, I'm going to save that for later. I'm not ruining your make-up now.' Standing by the bed, he pulled her hips back to meet his. He wrapped his arm around her waist, leaning over her to whisper in her ear. 'This way I can go deep, darling. Fill you up with my—'

'*Yes,*' she panted, excitement escalating despite the orgasm only seconds before. 'Please. I need you. Hard. Fill me—'

'Like this?' he rasped.

He slammed deep. She shuddered, bucked, then pushed back so he was locked to the absolute hilt.

'You feel *so* good, Bethan,' he choked.

But he kept control—teasing her with slow strokes, eking out her pleasure, loving her completely. But she rocked on all fours, harder and faster, demanding a faster, fiercer, pace.

'Bethan—'

'Please...*please*...'

His growl reverberated through her as his self-control snapped. He pumped, hard and fast and everything she needed. The force of his final thrust tumbled them both to the bed.

With a combination laugh and gasp he rolled her to her side. 'Oh, hell, your make-up!'

'I don't care,' she giggled.

'Because you've got what you wanted?' he murmured wolfishly. 'Honestly, you look so beautiful right now. I'm going to have to ravish you again as soon as all those guests leave.'

She pressed her hand to her belly. Whether it was instinct or wishful imagination, she had a sudden certainty that his seed had struck.

His eyebrows arched. 'You think?'

'It's possible, right?'

'Bethan.' He drew her close and tenderly pressed a

gentle kiss on the tip of her nose. 'With you, *anything* is possible.'

And sure enough, nine and a half months later their son arrived—impatient and demanding, loving and full of vitality—the perfect blend of them both.

* * * * *

If Greek Vows Revisited *left you wanting more, then don't miss the previous instalments in the Convenient Wives Club trilogy,* Their Altar Arrangement *and* Boss's Baby Acquisition! *And why not explore these other stories from Natalie Anderson?*

The Boss's Stolen Bride
Impossible Heir for the King
Back to Claim His Crown
My One-Night Heir
Billion-Dollar Dating Game

Available now!

Get up to 4 Free Books!

We'll send you 2 free books from each series you try PLUS a free Mystery Gift.

FREE Value Over **$25**

Both the **Harlequin Presents** and **Harlequin Medical Romance** series feature exciting stories of passion and drama.

YES! Please send me 2 FREE novels from Harlequin Presents or Harlequin Medical Romance and my FREE gift (gift is worth about $10 retail). After receiving them, if I don't wish to receive any more books, I can return the shipping statement marked "cancel." If I don't cancel, I will receive 6 brand-new larger-print novels every month and be billed just $7.19 each in the U.S., or $7.99 each in Canada, or 4 brand-new Harlequin Medical Romance Larger-Print books every month and be billed just $7.19 each in the U.S. or $7.99 each in Canada, a savings of 20% off the cover price. It's quite a bargain! Shipping and handling is just 50¢ per book in the U.S. and $1.25 per book in Canada.* I understand that accepting the 2 free books and gift places me under no obligation to buy anything. I can always return a shipment and cancel at any time. The free books and gift are mine to keep no matter what I decide.

Choose one:
- ☐ **Harlequin Presents Larger-Print** (176/376 BPA G36Y)
- ☐ **Harlequin Medical Romance** (171/371 BPA G36Y)
- ☐ **Or Try Both!** (176/376 & 171/371 BPA G36Z)

Name (please print)

Address   Apt. #

City   State/Province   Zip/Postal Code

Email: Please check this box ☐ if you would like to receive newsletters and promotional emails from Harlequin Enterprises ULC and its affiliates. You can unsubscribe anytime.

Mail to the Harlequin Reader Service:
IN U.S.A.: P.O. Box 1341, Buffalo, NY 14240-8531
IN CANADA: P.O. Box 603, Fort Erie, Ontario L2A 5X3

Want to explore our other series or interested in ebooks? Visit www.ReaderService.com or call 1-800-873-8635.

---

*Terms and prices subject to change without notice. Prices do not include sales taxes, which will be charged (if applicable) based on your state or country of residence. Canadian residents will be charged applicable taxes. Offer not valid in Quebec. This offer is limited to one order per household. Books received may not be as shown. Not valid for current subscribers to the Harlequin Presents or Harlequin Medical Romance series. All orders subject to approval. Credit or debit balances in a customer's account(s) may be offset by any other outstanding balance owed by or to the customer. Please allow 4 to 6 weeks for delivery. Offer available while quantities last.

Your Privacy—Your information is being collected by Harlequin Enterprises ULC, operating as Harlequin Reader Service. For a complete summary of the information we collect, how we use this information and to whom it is disclosed, please visit our privacy notice located at https://corporate.harlequin.com/privacy-notice. Notice to California Residents – Under California law, you have specific rights to control and access your data. For more information on these rights and how to exercise them, visit https://corporate.harlequin.com/california-privacy. For additional information for residents of other U.S. states that provide their residents with certain rights with respect to personal data, visit https://corporate.harlequin.com/other-state-residents-privacy-rights/.